Ink Exposed

A Montgomery Ink Novel

By
Carrie Ann Ryan

Author Highlights

Praise for Carrie Ann Ryan....

"Carrie Ann Ryan knows how to pull your heartstrings and make your pulse pound! Her wonderful Redwood Pack series will draw you in and keep you reading long into the night. I can't wait to see what comes next with the new generation, the Talons. Keep them coming, Carrie Ann!" –Lara Adrian, New York Times bestselling author of CRAVE THE NIGHT

"Carrie Ann Ryan never fails to draw readers in with passion, raw sensuality, and characters that pop off the page. Any book by Carrie Ann is an absolute treat." – New York Times Bestselling Author J. Kenner

"With snarky humor, sizzling love scenes, and brilliant, imaginative worldbuilding, The Dante's Circle series reads as if Carrie Ann Ryan peeked at my personal wish list!" – NYT Bestselling Author, Larissa Ione

"Carrie Ann Ryan writes sexy shifters in a world full of passionate happily-ever-afters." – *New York Times* Bestselling Author Vivian Arend

"Carrie Ann's books are sexy with characters you can't help but love from page one. They are heat and heart blended to perfection." *New York Times* Bestselling Author Jayne Rylon

Carrie Ann Ryan's books are wickedly funny and deliciously hot, with plenty of twists to keep you guessing. They'll keep you up all night!" USA Today Bestselling Author Cari Quinn

"Once again, Carrie Ann Ryan knocks the Dante's Circle series out of the park. The queen of hot, sexy, enthralling paranormal romance, Carrie Ann is an author not to miss!" *New York Times* bestselling Author Marie Harte

Dedication

For those who think they don't deserve an HEA.

Acknowledgements

It's time! Alex and Tabby's book is finally here. I've been eagerly anticipating this book since Delicate Ink back in 2014. I knew from the moment I wrote about an organized planner waiting in the wings that she'd be perfect for Alex. What's funny is that nine out of ten readers thought Tabby would end up with Storm or Wes...or even both!

I knew, though, that Tabby needed someone else. And Alex needed her even more.

Alex is an alcoholic. That is not a secret nor is the fact that his recovery has been hard. It has been over a year in terms of the characters' lives so Alex could have time just be him, and not worry about his love life. I purposely wrote it this way because most people say that recovering addicts need that time. I didn't want to rush him despite the fact that readers wanted his book ASAP.

I'm glad I didn't.

In order to write this book I couldn't have done it on my own. So thank you Team Carrie Ann for being amazing. Also, we need shirts that say this. I'm just saying.

Thank you Chelle for not only helping me plot, for editing my words so they made more sense than gibberish. Thank you Charity for being my right hand woman and being the best graphic artist and assistant ever. Thank you Tara for all the publicist and background work that go into each and every release. Thank you Avery Flynn, Kimberly Kincaid, Christi Barth, and Skye Jordan for not running away at the writing retreat when I said I wanted to write Alex's book and I had a plot idea. You ladies rock.

Thank you Dr. Hubby for not only understanding when I need to work some weekends, but for holding me when I started sobbing writing this book. And thank you so freaking much for being my formatter. You never get annoyed (at least to me!) when I say I need you to fix something in my backmatter...in 55 books.

I love you.

Thank you bloggers and reviewers for helping me spread the word. You guys help me so much with each release and your support matters beyond words.

As always, thank you dear readers for sticking with me and for new ones for finding me!

Happy reading!
~Carrie Ann

Ink Exposed

The Montgomery Ink series continues with the brother that deserves a second chance, and the woman who has always loved him.

Alex Montgomery lost his first love and then proceeded to leave himself in the bottle. Only he and his ex-wife truly know why he fell so hard and so fast down a path he never thought he'd take. Now he's clean, out of rehab, and learning how to be a Montgomery once again—a task that isn't quite as easy as some of his family assumes.

Tabby Collins is an honorary Montgomery and the organizational mastermind behind Montgomery Inc., the family's construction company. She loves her planners, friends, and a certain dark-haired man who's never given her a second glance.

Alex is slowly re-immersing himself back into the world, but the demons he faced before aren't out of the picture, and he'll have to learn to rely on others to make it out whole. When Alex discovers that Tabby's life is in danger, he not only finds a way to help her but also learns the true woman behind the soft smiles he's always seen. Their romance won't be an easy one, but nothing this passionate and heart-pounding ever is.

CHAPTER ONE

Alex Montgomery didn't need a drink.
But he fucking *craved* one.
This feeling wasn't new, of course. The craving was always there. It burned in his gut, spiraled up his spine, and parched his throat. It clawed at him, seduced him, rammed into him like it couldn't help itself. It was like an angry linebacker, screaming in one ear while a seductive temptress whispered sexy innuendos in the other, both of them telling him to just take one drink.

It would only be one drink, they taunted. *Just one.*

Only it never ended at one drink.

Because Alex was an alcoholic. He hadn't had a drink soothe his parched throat, or tried to drown his demons in over a year. He still couldn't quite believe it sometimes, and yet, other times it felt as if it had been so much longer. Sixteen months sober, but an addict nonetheless. No matter how many days passed and how many drinks he *didn't* imbibe, he'd always be an alcoholic. That was something he'd learned to face over the past few months, but sometimes knowing it didn't make trying to live a normal life any easier.

"You're here early," Marie Montgomery said as she made her way to his side. He'd been standing outside even in the cold Denver air, but his mother had found him anyway. He loved the scent of mountains and comfort that seemed to permeate his childhood home, and just looking at the woman who'd raised him made him feel that much closer to what he'd lost...and that much farther away from where he'd started.

His mother had aged well, he thought. To the point he wasn't sure she'd aged at all. If her genes were what the family could go by when they got older, then most of his siblings were going to look just fine as they entered their fifties and sixties. Alex had probably pickled his liver during his depression so he figured it probably wouldn't be quite the same for him. He'd more than likely end up harder-edged than his already edgy siblings. But that had been his choice at one point, and then out of his hands after he'd fallen too hard. Now, he'd face the consequences of his decisions. And it was about time he faced the aftermath according to his sponsor and therapist.

His mother wrapped her arms around his waist and held on tightly. He ignored the way his stomach tightened, and hugged her back, the action almost rusty. It hadn't been easy these past few months to remember how affectionate his family had once been with him. He'd pushed them all away over time, and he was just now learning how to come back—if there were a way to come back. When he closed his eyes and inhaled the scent that had once calmed him, he prayed that one day he'd find himself tranquil again.

He used to drink to forget, and then, because he didn't know anything else, he'd kept drinking. But now, he needed to remember, damn it.

He kissed the top of his mother's head since she was so much smaller than he was and took a step back. She was a few inches shorter than all of her sons and even a couple of inches shorter than her three daughters. How Marie Montgomery had been able to raise eight kids as well as all of their friends who'd come to their home day after day was beyond him.

"I'm glad you're here, though." She patted his chest and looked up at him with worried eyes. She always held that worry now; and he knew it was his fault that it was there.

"I wouldn't be anywhere else," he said honestly. His mother's eyes softened, and he figured he'd said the right thing. "I know the family dinner starts in a couple hours, but I wanted to come early and see if I could help." Though their family was considered huge in this day and age, the immediate family members all lived within thirty minutes of each other in the Denver suburbs. Some of them had moved away for a year or two for school or life, but they'd all come back to Denver in the end. Once he'd gotten out of rehab, he'd considered moving away and starting over, but he'd just be hurting those who had loved him through all his crap. They'd stayed with him, pushed him toward the decision he'd had to make for himself, and now, he was glad he'd stayed in the city.

At least, that's how he felt in that moment. With the way his mind kept going in a thousand different directions, he could change his mind again soon.

Since his parents were ecstatic that all of their babies were so close, they held family dinners twice a month. Sometimes, they made it happen more often; sometimes, they could only get everybody together

3

once, but all of Alex's siblings tried to make it when they could. Add in the fact that the rest of his family had been having children at an alarming rate recently, and their family dinners were always loud, full, and exhausting.

Once again, he ignored the tightening in his stomach.

I can do this, he told himself again.

He'd been normal once. He could try to at least play at being normal again.

"Anyway, you could have come right into the house, Alex," his mother continued. "You didn't have to come in through the backyard. You could have just come right in through the front door. No need to even knock since you're one of my babies. Since the chemo and radiation treatments are over, your father wasn't taking a nap like he used to."

Alex's father, Harry, had battled prostate cancer the year before when Alex had been going through his own self-induced downward spiral. Alex hadn't been in any shape to be the kind of son Harry needed when he'd faced death and won. Thankfully, Alex had four other brothers who were far stronger than he was, and three sisters who kicked ass at anything they did.

"I wanted to walk the long way before I made it inside." He shrugged, and she gave him a curious look. He sighed and pointed to one of the picnic tables on the large patio his father and his brother Austin had built over a decade ago. Austin was a few years older than Alex and had always been good with his hands. Yet it had been the next two siblings in the line, Wes and Storm, who had joined Harry in his construction company. While Austin had opened his own tattoo shop with their sister, Maya.

"I brought my camera in case you wanted photos or something and figured I'd see if anything caught my eye out here." He didn't look in her direction as he said it, suddenly self-conscious. He was a photographer and photojournalist by trade, but he'd lost many of his contacts when he found himself at the bottom of a bottle. He'd spent the past year trying to atone for his sins, making new connections and repairing the ones he'd broken, but he wasn't quite there yet.

His mother put her hand on his forearm, and he looked down at her again. "I think that would be wonderful. Nothing formal I suppose since we didn't warn anyone, but I'd love some shots of the family being who they are and just enjoying themselves. You were always talented at capturing that." Tears filled her eyes, and she blinked them away, though not fast enough for him not to feel like a heel for putting them there. "I look forward to seeing what you come up with. You're so talented."

He nodded, swallowing hard. Maybe one day he wouldn't feel like a stranger in the home he'd grown up in, but today wouldn't be that day. Hell, he felt like a stranger in his own skin, let alone allowing space for anyone else to see who he was.

He didn't even *know* who he was anymore.

"Mrs. Montgomery?"

Alex turned at the sound of the soft voice behind him, his heart suddenly beating just a bit faster, though he didn't know why.

Tabitha moved toward them, a hesitant smile on her face as she studied him and his mom. She wore her light auburn hair up high in a ponytail, but he was pretty sure at one point she'd been blonde. Though it might have just been a trick of the light. If he were honest with himself, he couldn't quite remember much of the past couple of years. She was a little above average height and all legs—legs he'd checked out more than once in the past year.

But he'd always pushed those thoughts aside, just as he would now. He was in recovery, damn it, and though he was past the year mark that most people suggested addicts wait to start a relationship, he knew that Tabitha wouldn't be the woman he started up with once he was ready.

She worked with his brothers, Storm and Wes, at Montgomery Inc. She was the administrative assistant for the construction company his parents had started before he was born, and he was pretty sure she ran the company with utmost efficiency. Wes might be super organized and diligent, but Alex knew Wes and Storm wouldn't be able to function without Tabitha.

"Tabby!" His mother moved forward and brought the other woman into her arms.

Tabitha smiled fondly, this time not as hesitantly, and hugged his mother back. "Hi, Mrs. Montgomery. I thought I'd come a bit early and see if you needed help cooking today. Mr. Montgomery let me in and I saw you guys out here through the window."

Alex stuffed his hands into his pockets and watched the way his mother fawned over Tabitha. He couldn't really blame her either. There wasn't a bad bone in Tabitha's body, and every time he saw her, she was always put together and helping someone. He didn't know if she had anyone at home waiting for her or family around here, but he knew the Montgomerys had taken her in anyway. They tended to do that to anyone they liked and admired who came near enough to their web.

"How many times have I asked you to call me Marie, Tabby?" Marie held Tabitha's hands and shook her head, though he could tell his mother was smiling.

"Every time I see you. But I have a bad habit I can't seem to shake." Tabitha looked up and over at Alex and smiled, though it wasn't the same smile she'd given his mother, and he couldn't quite read it. "Hi, Alexander."

"Hi." He always found it weird that they were the only ones who called each other by their full names but it had been one of those things that had stuck years ago, and he didn't know how to change it. And frankly, he didn't want to.

"Anyway, it's Storm's turn to help me in the kitchen if you want to join me," Marie put in. "The rest of the kids and their babies will be here a bit later." She looked over her shoulder. "Alex, honey, grab your camera and come inside. If you're bored, you can help us start cooking."

His stomach did that tightening thing again at the thought of being included, but this time, it didn't hurt. No, it was more a warmth he couldn't quite place. He kind of liked it.

"I can do that," he said softly then went back to get his camera. He jogged to the picnic table and picked up his bag. His hands shook, and he forced himself to take a deep breath and count to ten.

"Are you okay?"

He turned on his heel, his eyes widening. He hadn't heard Tabitha came up behind him, and he swallowed hard, his heart racing. "Yeah, just picking up my camera."

She tilted her head, studying his face. "Okay. Your mom went into the kitchen to get her lists. Storm will be here in a few minutes, apparently. I hope you don't mind that I came early to help out. I didn't know you'd be here ahead of time, as well, and I didn't mean to break up whatever you and your mom were planning."

He quickly shook his head as he placed the strap of his bag on his shoulder. He kept fiddling with it since, for some reason, he wanted to reach out and touch her in order to reassure her. He didn't need to be touching Tabitha in any way.

"You didn't interrupt anything." He gave a dry laugh, and she gave him a curious look. "You're part of the family now, you know. If anything, I bet you're more of a Montgomery than I am these days." He hadn't meant to say the latter, and could have kicked himself once the words were out. He hadn't meant to open up like that.

She didn't give him a pitying look, however. Instead, she narrowed her eyes. "You're a Montgomery, even if you don't think of it that way right now. You've always been a Montgomery and not just in name." She let out a breath, and the two of them stood in an awkward silence. "Anyway, we should get going so we can help out." She turned on her heel, and he let out a breath of his own before he followed her.

He didn't know what it was about Tabitha Collins that had made him open up even that little bit just then, but he wasn't sure he wanted to find out anytime soon.

When they got inside, Storm was just walking in through the front door, a large smile on his face. Storm and Wes were fraternal twins so they didn't look exactly alike, but out of all the Montgomerys, they looked the *most* alike. All of them had dark hair and blue eyes, and most of them had ink and piercings, as well. Considering a couple of his siblings owned and operated a tattoo shop, it only made sense. They made for an eclectic bunch, but they were Montgomerys so that's all that mattered.

Or, at least, that's all that *should* have mattered until Alex kicked all of that to the curb.

He shook off those thoughts and went to greet Storm. The two of them did that man hug thing he never truly understood but did anyway before they headed into the kitchen. Storm hugged Tabitha close before kissing her on the top of the head and getting to work.

"Is that how you treat your staff at work, dear?" Marie asked with a twinkle in her eyes. Alex was pretty sure Marie wanted Tabitha married into the Montgomery clan, and figured either Wes or Storm would do.

Alex didn't count, after all.

Storm winked and kissed his mother's cheek. "Only outside of work, Mom. Don't worry."

Tabitha blushed and waved them off. "If they tried it at the office, I'd kick their butts. Don't worry."

"It's true," Storm said as he searched through the fridge. "She could take all of us."

Alex raised a brow. "Good to know."

If it were possible, Tabitha blushed even harder before going back to work. Alex held back a frown at the reaction and set down his camera case before his mother put him to work, as well. As long as he wasn't at home sitting alone and trying to think of something to do, he'd take whatever came next.

It took a couple of hours, but they eventually had the meal ready to go. His mom had wanted to go Italian tonight so they had a couple of pans of lasagna, an Alfredo dish, as well as pasta with meatballs for the kids. They'd even made salads, side dishes, and antipasto. Since there were eight siblings, and most of them had significant others, as well as children *and* people like Tabitha who had been practically adopted in, that added up. There were a lot of mouths to feed.

But the Montgomerys sure knew how to take care of each other even if they were only talking about their stomachs this time.

His mother had been in charge of desserts so he knew there would be tons of sweet goodness after the main meal, as well. He rubbed a hand over his stomach and sighed. He wasn't sure he'd have room for dessert in the end, and he didn't want to overindulge. He'd done that enough in his life.

As the rest of the family began to arrive, he pulled out his camera. This wasn't his first family meal since he'd gotten out of rehab, but he still wasn't up to the full strength needed to deal with the entire lot of them at once.

His family loved him. He knew that. They were the ones who'd forced him to look at himself and had been there to pick up the pieces when he'd fallen apart. He hadn't been strong enough to do it alone, and while he didn't resent them for it, he did resent himself.

It was easier to be behind the lens and take photos of his family interacting than it was to actually be part of it. While he was still *there,* he could step away and be an observer.

He focused on one side of the room, snapping a few photos as his sister Meghan threw her head back and laughed at something her husband Luc said. Luc held their daughter, Emma, in his arms. The little girl was about five months old now if he was counting right. In fact, his three sisters had each given birth to a child five months ago, which just went to show how close the Montgomerys were. They even bred on a similar schedule so their children could grow up together. Though he knew they hadn't done it on purpose, it was still a little weird.

His other sister, Maya, leaned back against one of her husbands, Border, while their third, Jake, held their son, Noah. Beside them, Miranda, Alex's final sister, held her son, Micah, while her husband, Decker, stood to the side of them, smiling like a proud papa.

Alex continued to take photos, ignoring the ache in his chest at the sight of all of his family members finding their own paths and making families of their own.

He'd fucked up the family he had, and knew he wouldn't be getting a second chance. His ex-wife was long gone, thankfully, and he wasn't about to fall into that trap again.

He didn't figure he was strong enough to do it a second time.

Once again, he pushed those thoughts from his mind and kept taking photos. Griffin and Autumn cuddling in the corner. Austin and Sierra wrangling heir brood in the center of the room. His parents dancing to the delight of Tabitha, Storm, and Wes. With each click of the shutter, he captured the memory for eternity without actually living it himself.

It was what he did, though, and he'd be damned if he failed at this one thing.

The timer went off behind him, and he turned as his mother clapped her hands, signaling the troops. "Okay, crew, find your seats. Storm and Alex? Come help me put the food out on the table."

When his mother spoke, people listened, so he put away his camera and went to place the plates of food on the table. Each sibling took their turn acting as sous chef and waitstaff, so Alex took his role in stride. Thankfully, those talented with building things with their own two hands in his family had built a large banquet table to fit everyone at once. Though he figured with all the children popping up everywhere, it would be a tight fit soon.

Eventually, he found himself seated next to Jake on one side, and his nephew, Austin's son, Leif, on the other. Tabitha sat in front of him with Storm and Wes on either side of her. While his mother hadn't put out place cards, he had a feeling she'd had a hand in that particular seating arrangement. His mom *really* wanted Tabitha as part of the family.

Everyone piled their plates high with food, though he was very careful to only take small portions of each dish. Everything was so carb and fat rich, and he had to be careful and not gorge himself. It wasn't that he didn't want to eat everything, but now that he didn't have drinking to binge on, and had never turned to smoking, he was afraid he'd overindulge with food. Too many of those in his program had done that, and he didn't want to trade one vice for another. His therapist was okay with the way he policed himself for now, but Alex knew he would always be balancing on the line of obsession and a new addiction.

"Did you get enough?" Leif asked from Alex's side. The kid was almost a teenager now, which scared the hell out of his dad, as well as Alex. "I can reach the Alfredo if you want more."

Alex shook his head. "I'm good. I have enough on my plate. Thank you."

Leif shrugged. "You're welcome."

"You sure you're eating enough?" Storm asked, and Alex narrowed his eyes.

"Yep. I promise." His tone must not have been as smooth as he'd have liked because the others went a bit quiet around him. "I'm eating plenty, I promise." And he was, though he'd eaten more in the past. But now that he was working out more, he'd added additional protein to his diet and not carbs. He hated that he even had to justify it, but he'd messed everything up before by becoming an alcoholic so he figured his family might not trust him to take care of himself anymore.

Not that he blamed them.

He didn't entirely trust himself.

Everyone continued to eat and talk, and Alex spoke quietly with Jake and some of the others when they asked him questions. He still wasn't completely comfortable so it was easier to sit and observe rather than participate.

"Hey, I might have a job for you if you're interested," Storm said, breaking Alex out of his thoughts.

"Really?" he asked. He needed the money, and if Storm could help him find a legitimate job, then he'd take it. He didn't want handouts, but he'd work for it.

"Yeah. Actually, it was Wes and Tabby's idea."

Alex turned to the others, his brows raised.

Tabby blushed, but Wes was the one who answered. "We're redoing the website, and we want to have a couple of printed books to hand out and for the office. Hardbound for the office, but I don't know yet about the other printed materials. We want to focus on what we're good at and show off what we've done. Storm and I could easily snap a few photos, but they wouldn't be anywhere near as good as what you do."

"We'd pay you your normal fee, too," Storm added. "It's not like we'd expect you to just do it for us because you're family."

Alex frowned. "But you *should* expect that."

"Uh, no," Maya put in. "You all pay for your ink when you come into the shop."

"And I get paid for doing work with Montgomery Inc. even though I'm family," Meghan said softly. "We

13

all work together *because* we're family, but we need to make a living, as well."

Alex swallowed hard, aware that everyone was looking at him. He felt exposed, raw, but he ignored it. He'd felt even more exposed before when he'd tried to drink himself to death, only this time, he didn't have the booze to numb it all.

"I think I can do that. Just tell me what you want."

He didn't miss the way his mother reached for his father's hand, and the two of them looked at him as if he'd made a giant leap.

He let out a breath and tried to ignore the stares. Finally, it was Tabitha who made a noise, breaking the tension. She yelped as she reached out for her water, spilling it on her lap and some of the table. "Oops! Sorry!"

She winked at him, but he wasn't sure anyone else had noticed. He stood up to help her, but Storm and Wes were already on the case. He didn't know why Tabitha had done that and taken the heat off him, but he sure was grateful. Soon, the others went back to what they were doing, and Tabitha came out with a new glass and more napkins.

When they were finished eating, everyone took their plates to the kitchen and picked up more drinks if needed. Alex pulled out a soda. Though he didn't need the sugar, he wanted the caffeine and wasn't in the mood for coffee.

Austin and Wes pulled out beers for themselves while in the middle of a conversation about Wes's next tattoo. When Austin popped the top, the sound echoed at just the right frequency within the kitchen so that everyone heard it. In fact, every single person froze where they were and turned mortified looks toward Alex.

For the first few dinners, everyone had stayed away from drinking around him, but he'd hated that. None of his family members had ever abused alcohol and had always been really careful about who was driving even after one drink. He'd eventually convinced them to start drinking what they wanted, but it hadn't been easy. Alcohol wasn't evil, but Alex didn't know how to say no after one or two drinks. It wasn't within him to do so, and therefore, he had to stay away from it entirely. But after a long day where his family worked until sweat soaked through their shirts at their demanding jobs, if they wanted a simple beer, then damn it, they deserved it.

And he'd learned to live with it.

One step at a time.

In response to the stares, he deliberately opened his soda slowly, the pop of the top echoing just as much as Austin's beer had. The tension in the room popped like a balloon, and he could practically see everyone take a deep breath as one.

One day, he figured he might be forgiven for how he'd betrayed his family, but it wouldn't be anytime soon. He'd broken their trust, and he'd broken himself in the process.

His gaze met Tabitha's across the kitchen, and she swallowed hard, her eyes wide. He deliberately turned away and headed into the living room where some of the others were. He didn't deserve to look at Tabitha that way. She was too sweet, too innocent for a man like him.

She deserved someone who hadn't carved his path through the world with a broken bottle. And he deserved...well, he wasn't sure what he deserved, but it wasn't her.

It would never be her.

CHAPTER TWO

Tabby Collins lit her two large, fat candles and smiled. There was nothing like getting ready for an evening just for herself. It felt *indulgent*. And if there was one thing Tabby was not, it was indulgent. But after the day she'd had, she would take this moment.

The candles lent a warm glow to the dark wood shine of her desk, and she sighed before turning on the lamp next to her computer. She needed a little more light to do what she had to do next, but the organic wax candles she'd bought on a whim sent off a nice scent that put her in the right mood.

She turned on her music to low and swayed back and forth to the beat as she poured herself a glass of wine. Just a small glass since she still needed to focus as well as wake up early tomorrow for work, but a nice glass of Malbec after a day like today was needed. When she was sure everything was in place, she set her glass down next to her workspace and stretched her arms over her head. She'd come home from working at Montgomery Inc. that evening and had immediately put on her comfy leggings and tank. They were softer than her winter pajamas, and if she could get away with it, she'd have worn them to work every day. What would the Montgomerys say if she showed up in leggings with unicorns on them and a bright pink tank with tiny white hearts decorating the seams? They so didn't match her normal work attire—pencil skirts, day dresses, slender slacks—and she was just fine with that.

Her body thrumming with the gentle, sweet taste of her wine and the music surrounding her, she sank into her desk chair and sighed.

While some women might turn on music and light candles to relax or even pleasure themselves, Tabby was going to find her own form of bliss.

With a soft smile, she cracked open her weekly planner. She'd spent far too much money on the accessories for it, and even though her life was also on her digital calendar, she needed to write down her daily to-do list for the next day as well as ensure she'd checked off the current day's list. There was nothing quite like checking something off her to-do list. It was almost euphoric. The other women in her planner group online felt the same as she did, so she knew she wasn't completely alone in her...addiction, but she still didn't advertise her love of planners, journals, and pens in public.

She had a feeling Wes Montgomery might know since she figured he had a planner of his own, but other than that, this time, and this thick notebook filled with her goals and lists was just for her.

She opened her washi tape container and thought about what color would work for the next two days. Since she worked with a paper planner that showed her each day at a time, she tended to color coordinate by two-day periods. Yes, she was crazy, and a little obsessive, but this was what made her happy so everyone else would just have to deal with it.

She quickly finished adding the colors she wanted for the next two days so she could focus and opened her digital calendar to make sure she didn't miss anything. Just writing things down soothed her and ensured she didn't miss an appointment or upcoming bill with a client.

Montgomery Inc. counted on her, and she would not fail them. The others joked that the Montgomerys couldn't keep going with all they did within the company without her, but she knew it was a team effort. If her OCD organizational techniques helped them in any way, then she'd take it.

Tapping her foot to the music, she added a few notes for the next day concerning Wes and Storm. The twins ran the construction company, while their sister, Meghan, had joined recently in the landscape development arm. And Tabby made sure all three of them—as well as the rest of the staff and crew—knew where they had to be and when. And when she wasn't doing that, Tabby worked with the clients firsthand on billing, timing, and other matters that the others couldn't deal with. She loved her job, and felt that she kicked ass at it.

But she needed this planner to make sure she could do it all.

After she had taken another sip of her wine, she added a few notes about a new client meeting the next day, as well as a sticker to remind her to call her mother and at least one of her three brothers.

She paused, laughing at herself.

Okay, so maybe adding a special sticker to remind herself to actually call her family out in Pennsylvania was a little over the top, but she'd loved the little stickers when she saw them online, and had now found a use for them. A crazy use, but a use nonetheless.

Shaking her head, she finished up her massive to-do list for the next two days and sipped the last of her wine. She missed her family, but the Montgomerys had taken her in as soon as she'd taken the entry-level job at Montgomery Inc. She not only worked with them during the week and sometimes even on weekends, but she went to many of their weekend family dinners, as well. At first, she'd felt a little out of place, but the massively inked and pierced Montgomerys hadn't let her feel that way for long.

Every single one of them had made her feel like part of the family. Well, maybe not all of them. Alexander had always been a little distant with her—especially when he'd been married and on his downward spiral—but he had been different since he'd gotten out of rehab.

She frowned, standing up so she could clean her workspace before she got ready for bed. Alexander was different with everyone since he'd been working toward his sobriety. She wasn't special in his new attentions, and she would do well to remember that. Just because she'd had a crush—or maybe something stronger than that—on him for years, didn't mean he had any feelings for her in that way. In fact, it would be better if he didn't. He was doing so well now, and she refused to do anything to jeopardize that.

Alexander Montgomery needed time to heal, and Tabby wasn't a part of that.

She'd never been part of it. And that was just fine with her. Or it would have to be.

Her phone rang then, cutting into her music and the dangerous road her thoughts had gone down.

When she checked the readout, she smiled again. "Hey, Dare. I was just thinking about you."

Her eldest brother chuckled. Though she could hear the sounds of the bar he owned in the background, he must have been off in a private corner since she could hear him pretty clearly. "Adding me into your planner, then?" he teased.

She huffed. "If you were closer, I'd punch you."

"If you were closer, you'd live in Pennsylvania with the rest of the family and make our poor mother's heart burst at the seams with happiness," he said dryly.

She winced at the familiar argument. She'd moved to Colorado for college when she'd gotten a full ride at the University of Colorado - Denver thanks to her grades. It wasn't the largest university in the state, but she'd wanted to move away from her small town and live in the large city next to mountains that seemed out of this world. Her three older brothers had stayed behind, though they'd gotten even more overprotective in their grumbling.

"You're laying it on pretty thick, Dare."

He sighed. "Sorry. Had a hard day at work and figured I'd call you this week instead of you calling me. Just wanted to hear your voice and make sure those Montgomerys were treating you right."

Tabby's shoulders relaxed as soon as he said the words, and she smiled softly as they talked. Though they were hundreds of miles away from each other, she was still as close to her family as she had been when she was living in the same small town. Dare, Fox, and Loch had babied her since the time she'd come home from the hospital, and her parents had let them. She'd been fiercely protected, loved, and adored.

And, to be honest, a little stifled. But now that she had a little distance, she knew it had been because of love and not anything else.

After she'd hung up with Dare, she cleaned up her living room and headed into her master bedroom, knowing she didn't have as much time to take a bath as she'd planned. A short soak to work out the kinks and de-stress would have to be enough.

She turned on the tap and added a bath bomb that turned the water a fizzy purple that smelled of lavender and lemon. While that was going, she stripped off her clothes and piled her long hair on top of her head before putting a mud mask on her face. If she were going to relax for fifteen minutes, she might as well go all out.

As she stared at herself in the mirror, she did her best to think about relaxing and not about the thoughts that had been worming their way into her mind once again.

She needed to go back and search for them.

No, she told herself. She couldn't continue to look and not only keep herself safe but also keep her sanity intact. It killed her little by little each time she searched for them and came up empty.

Tabby let out a breath and gripped the edge of the counter.

Stop it. Stop it.

With a groan, she pushed herself away and forced those thoughts out of her brain as she slid into the bathtub. She turned off the taps and made herself rest her head on the edge of the tub. She would relax before she went to bed, and then she'd wake up and work like she always did.

There would be no more searching for those she'd lost.

An image of deep blue eyes that were just as lost filled her brain, and she cursed.

And there would be no more thinking about Alexander Montgomery either.

But when she finally got into bed and rested her head on her pillow, she failed on at least one of those things. Alexander filled her dreams until she woke up exhausted, sweaty, and aching for something she couldn't have.

How freaking embarrassing.

"Do you have the file on the Laymont place?" Wes asked as he frowned over his tablet. "I have it here but I think something's missing."

"Maybe if you didn't spend all your time on your precious tablet and more time with a hammer in your hand, you wouldn't feel like you were losing things," Storm said dryly from his desk.

Tabby, used to their banter, quickly pulled out the backup paper file from the cabinet and walked it over to Wes. "Nothing's missing in the online file. I just checked it. But the owners haven't decided on the last requirements so we were waiting on that before proceeding. Remember?"

Wes pinched the bridge of his nose as he took the folder from her. "Hell. I knew that. What is wrong with me? I'm usually on point better than this."

Tabby shook her head and went to the coffee maker they kept in their offices. They had an open floor plan for the five of them—Wes, Storm, Tabby, Decker, and Meghan—and while they kept a break room for everyone with an additional coffee maker, Tabby had found it best to keep the caffeine closer to the Montgomerys at all times. Soon, they would be adding a sixth desk once the new guy, Harper, was ready to move in, and she would have to figure out how to make that work, as well. It was rare for all five of them to be in the office at the same time since most of them worked on the project sites, but when they were all there, tension usually followed.

She quickly made Wes a cup of coffee as well as one for Storm since she was there and handed them over. While it wasn't exactly in her job description anymore to make them coffee, she couldn't help herself. Plus, it was better for everyone if the Montgomerys stayed caffeinated.

"We just added on four new projects when we usually only add one or two at a time," Tabby said smoothly. "The Gallaghers took up that restoration project we passed on because, frankly, that's their gig and not ours as much anymore, but we're still over capacity. That's why you hired Harper, though he hasn't started yet since he had to finish up his old project before he could start here. You're working on a hundred different things at once, and you keep forgetting that I'm here to help you so you're trying to do my work, as well. Not to mention the fact that you neglected to let Decker do his part on the Henderson house at first and put him in a bind because you felt the need to micromanage—something you don't usually do with Decker. He's our lead contractor and your brother-in-law and damn good at his job, but for some reason, you're freaking out about it. So why don't you sit down at your desk since your pacing is putting *me* on edge, drink your coffee, and check out the four to-do lists I left for you. They're color coded just as you like."

Wes sipped his coffee and stared at her over the brim of his mug. When he lowered his arm, he narrowed his eyes. "You know, people used to think *I* was the brains behind Montgomery Inc. Now, I'm thinking you took over my job."

"Hey, I'm sitting right here, you know," Storm said dryly from his worktable. Though he'd joked with

Wes about being on the computer all the time, Storm tended to do many of his designs on software.

She rolled her eyes. "Shut up. We all do our parts, and if we work together, it's not that scary. When you try to do everything, you get buried. And I don't mean just you. I mean all of us."

Wes went back to his desk and plopped down on his chair. "I hate it when you're right."

Tabby blinked quickly and made sure her face looked just a bit confused. "Oh, poor baby. You must hate it often, then."

Storm barked out a laugh as Tabby ducked from the flying ball of Post Its aimed at her head. Wes had decent aim, so she figured he'd missed on purpose. Working with Wes and Storm made it easier day by day to be so far away from her family.

She went back to work, answering phone calls and going through bills as the brothers joked with each other. It was still early in the day, and she knew more people would be dropping in and out of the building throughout the work shift. Montgomery Inc. was one of the top construction companies in Denver. They worked all over the city and each of the suburbs, putting up new buildings and repairing old ones. They did upgrades on smaller homes, as well as new builds on larger office buildings. The one thing they hadn't tackled yet was a skyscraper since that wasn't in their division, but she had a feeling if the Montgomerys had the means, they'd see it as a challenge and make one kickass high-rise.

While they worked in one room most of the time while they were in the building, they had other offices as well if they needed privacy or had to meet with clients. She loved the layout and never felt like she wasn't part of the team or as if she were lower than the others.

A little before lunch, the front door opened, and Meghan, Decker, and Harper made their way in.

"It's freezing outside, and yet there isn't a single flake of snow," Meghan said with a sigh as she peeled off her outer layer of clothes. "I mean, it's supposed to be winter, and yet we've only had two snow storms."

"And since it's Denver, it usually just melts a few hours later," Decker added. "That's good for us, though. More work on the outsides of the buildings. And since you literally work with dirt, it not being frozen is a good thing."

Tabby smiled and tilted her head in hello as everyone went to their desks. Well, not everyone. Harper didn't have a desk yet since he technically didn't work for Montgomery Inc. for another couple of weeks. Officially anyway.

"Hello, Harper."

Harper tilted his chin. "Hi, Tabby. I have the rest of the paperwork you needed. Thought I'd drop it off before I head back out to my site."

He handed over a stack of papers, and she smiled, taking them from him. He could have used the digital booklets she'd set up, but a lot of these guys liked paper more. They all worked with their hands for a living so it only made sense.

"Thank you," she said and gave the papers a quick glance. "You should be all set once I go through all of this. Welcome to Montgomery Inc."

Storm came up at that point and put his hand on Harper's shoulder, giving it a squeeze. "Welcome, man. We're glad to have you."

"Hell, yeah," Decker put in, running a hand over his beard. "I'm glad you're coming in to help, man." Harper would work directly with Decker so they could parallel each other when the time came. Decker was the lead contractor but they needed a second so Wes didn't have to run himself ragged plugging up the holes.

"You guys are the best," Harper said simply. "I want to work with the best."

"Damn straight," Wes said with wink.

"You know what we really need," Decker said after a moment. "A new plumber. Harrison retired last fall, and having to schedule with contracted companies is killing our timetables."

Tabby took notes as they spoke, though it wasn't a full meeting. She always took notes in case someone said something that needed to be taken care of right away or even later and they happened to forget. And as she was the one who helped with the scheduling, she knew they were in desperate need of an in-house plumber.

"I can go through our files and see who we could reach out to. You have anyone in mind?" Tabby offered.

Storm opened his mouth to say something, but paused.

"What?" Wes asked. "You thinking of someone?"

Storm shook his head. "Maybe. No. Not really."

Tabby shared a look with Wes. Well, that wasn't cryptic at all. Before Storm could elaborate on his weird statement, the door opened again, and Alexander walked inside. Goosebumps broke out over Tabby's arms, and she held back a shiver. Damn it. She used to be better about keeping her facade when it came to him, but ever since he'd come back—a little quieter and a little more introspective—she hadn't been able to focus like she should.

"Hey!" Storm said with an easy smile on his face. "You came."

Alexander stuffed his hands in the pockets of his coat, pushing the camera bag he carried back just a bit. He rocked on his heels and stared at everyone, a little cautious. The room had gone quiet when he'd walked in, and Tabby had a feeling he hated that.

"You asked me to," he said softly. "If it's not a good time, I can come back later."

Wes moved forward. "You're always welcome. It's a family company, after all."

Something stark flashed over Alexander's face, and Tabby gripped her pen hard enough to leave an indent on her fingers. "So, what do you need?"

Storm cleared his throat. "I don't know exactly. I figured we'd give you free rein on what you think would work. Tabby would probably be the one to talk to since she knows where everyone is located at all times, or at least close to it."

Alexander met her gaze, and she forced herself not to flush—or at least she tried to. It wasn't like she could actually control that particular body function.

"Sounds like a plan," he said roughly.

"Let's go to one of the office rooms and I'll show you what we had in mind."

Tabby stood up quickly and gripped her planner—her lifeline—before making her way to him. And though she'd walked through the room countless times before in the heels she wore, the front of her left foot hit the hardwood at just the right spot—or wrong spot depending on how you looked at it.

She tripped, her hands flailing out in front of her. Her planner shot out one way, her pens the other. The others called out to her, and though everything happened in seconds, she could hear each individual voice and see the panicked look in Alexander's eyes.

Before she hit the ground, though, strong arms wrapped around her and brought her to a hard chest. She grunted as the breath got knocked out of her, and she slid her feet along the floor until she found her balance. Alexander held her firmly to him, his head lowered. She looked up at him, mortified.

"Uh, thank you."

"You okay?" His voice was low, a bit gruff, and did such horrible things to her. She wanted to press herself flush to his chest and take a bite out of his chin.

And that was *not* Tabitha Collins.

She didn't drape herself around a man and swoon like some Regency heroine.

Screw that.

She pulled herself away and straightened her clothes. "Thanks for catching me. I seem to like making an entrance...even after I'm already in the room." Storm had picked up her planner, and she took it from him, resisting the urge to clutch it to her chest and make sure it was unharmed.

"So, now that I've shown you my graceful walking skills, let's head over to the office." She turned on her heel—carefully this time—and strode toward the rooms in the back, careful not to make eye contact.

She'd just made a fool of herself in front of the man her heart refused to forget, and now she had to work with him on this next project. Closely.

It seemed today was going to be a very long day. Very long.

CHAPTER THREE

Alex held back a wince as his brother, Austin, dug in deeper, working on the shading part of his new tattoo. He was on his side, Austin hovering over him as his older brother finished up the last of the tree design they'd been working on along Alex's ribs. It might be cliché to want a symbol of rebirth and growth on his body, but it had been done countless times before for a reason.

He was trying to be a new man while attempting to remember where his roots needed to grow so he could stand up straight against the fierce and gaping hollowness that had been his past.

"Need a break?" Austin asked as he wiped down some of the ink, blood, and plasma that had seeped out with each passing wave of the needle.

"We're almost done, aren't we?" Alex asked. He sucked in a breath as Austin went over a particularly tender part of his ribs. While most people usually hit the point of the inking process where euphoria set in, Austin had stopped tattooing right when Alex had passed the point of pain and entered into that buzz. Alex didn't want any connection to the buzz, the happiness that came from getting a tattoo—not when he could go too far and make a mistake.

Ink was an addiction for some people, and Alex couldn't afford another craving.

"We are," Austin rumbling, continuing his work. "I just don't like seeing you wince."

Alex chuckled softly, trying not to move while Austin did his work. "I thought all big brothers liked picking on little ones."

Austin grinned then, a flash of white under that big beard of his. "Yeah, and you're the littlest of all my brothers, so you would think that'd be my goal. But, nah, I like you guys too much to want to keep punching the lot of you, especially since I'm over forty now."

Alex was the youngest son of the Montgomery clan. Only Miranda was younger among the eight of them. Yet other than Meghan and her first marriage, he had been married the longest before his divorce. He'd been young, just nineteen, and an idiot when he'd gotten married. Now he felt far older than his years—divorced, broken, and a hell of a lot stronger than he was before.

Or maybe that was weaker.

He just didn't know anymore.

"How's Austin doing?" Maya asked as she made her way over to them. She smiled down at him without her usual smirk, and he wanted to sigh. He missed that smirk—the one she gave the rest of her siblings as a sign of love. Oh, Maya might still love him, but she was always so damn careful around him. All of them were.

Yet he couldn't blame them.

"All done," Austin said. "He's just fine, Maya. You're just jealous that he came to me instead of you."

Alex grinned as Maya flipped him off. The two owned and operated Montgomery Ink and always fought over who got to tattoo their friends and family. Like the rest of his siblings, he took turns between them, and it just happened that his first tattoo since he'd gotten out of rehab was Austin's. The fact that it was also his biggest one had to annoy Maya, so he figured, at some point, he'd go through the whole ordeal again on the other side of his ribcage. He was going to end up with an entire body full of ink one day—just like the rest of them.

Austin helped Alex sit up and rolled his shoulders. "You know the after-care routine, but let's go through it anyway."

Alex listened as he stood up to take a look at his new ink in the long mirror Austin had in his station. This had been their second and final session, and he would forever be in awe of his brother's talent.

"Holy hell, man. You do good work."

Austin came up beside him so both of them were visible in the mirror. "Of course, I do good work. Why the fuck would you think I'd give you shit ink?"

Maya came up beside him and hip-checked him. He stood between his two siblings as they studied his new art, and a little part of his chest relaxed marginally. Each of them had the same brown hair, the same blue eyes, the same look of a Montgomery. He hadn't felt like one in far too long, but having these two standing on either side of him like this? Maybe he could do this. Maybe he could be...normal. Or whatever *normal* he could be.

"You could have had a bad day you know," Alex drawled. "One slip, and suddenly the tree on my side looks like a burned down forest or something."

Austin narrowed his eyes as Maya grinned like a loon. "Say that again, and maybe I'll draw that

31

unicorn on your ass that I threatened you with when you turned eighteen and snuck out late to make out with—"

Alex let out a breath through his nose and did his best to make sure his face looked as if he weren't feeling the hit to the solar plexus. He and Jessica had been high school sweethearts, dumb and in love and doing their best to ignore everyone else *and* their own issues. They'd had sex way too young, and they hadn't been ready for the consequences. They'd been so wrapped up in one another; they'd missed the fact that they didn't even like each other deep down. He'd snuck out of his house countless times, worrying his parents to no end just so he could have her for the night. She'd been his everything.

His first addiction.

Because of his need for her, he'd forgone college and picked up his camera so he could focus on his own version of studies. What he'd really done was throw his mind and body into Jessica and their sham of a marriage while taking odd jobs here and there until he'd hit it big enough with his own natural talent to create a life for the two of them. It had taken him a while to understand how to nurture that talent, and now he was trying to do it again.

He couldn't blame anyone but himself for the road he'd taken, but he knew there had been triggers.

And his ex-wife was one of them.

"I snuck out more than you thought I did," Alex said, cutting into the tension. "Of course, sometimes, it was just to watch you make out with whatever girl you were with at that time."

Austin growled. "Excuse me?"

Alex grinned this time, warm memories washing over him. "Griffin and I used to sneak out even before Griff got his license and we'd spy on you since we figured you knew what you were doing, and we'd learn a few things."

Maya cackled at his side as Austin turned on him. "I didn't even live with you guys when you two were old enough to do that kind of shit."

Alex laughed. "We figured out where you were from Shep and the twins. Then we followed you." Shep was their cousin that now lived in New Orleans, while Wes and Storm were the next in age after Austin.

"Little brothers, Austin. You have too many of them it seems."

Austin narrowed his eyes. "Hell. Just don't teach Leif or Conner any of that shit."

"They're going to find out anyway," Alex put in. "With the way you guys are popping kids out, there's going to be a whole new generation of Montgomerys, running around and acting crazy."

Bile filled his mouth as soon as he said the words but he swallowed it down. They didn't know, *couldn't* know. The others couldn't see.

"Anyway, I need to go. I have an appointment. Am I good?"

His siblings shared a look at his abrupt change in tone, but he ignored it. He might like that they had been starting to treat him normally again, but he couldn't let them see everything.

He couldn't.

"You're all ready to go as soon as I seal you up," Austin said cautiously. The conversation was stilted after that, but he couldn't blame anyone but himself. He kissed his sister on the forehead as he left and waved at Austin, keeping his emotions in check. Between thinking about Jessica, and, well...everything else, he was riding an edge he couldn't quite deal with.

He needed a damn drink.

But he wasn't going to have one.

Not now.

Not in an hour.

And damn well not tomorrow.

He pulled into the gym, his body tense as hell, and his hands clenched on the steering wheel. He hadn't lied to his brother and sister when he'd said he had an appointment, but it wasn't with his sponsor or a doctor like they probably thought. His meeting wasn't until tomorrow, so for now, he would release the tension riding him the only way he knew how.

Fighting it the fuck out of his system.

Brody and Harper were already in the locker room when he showed up, his gear over his shoulder. They gave him a look when he walked in, and he shrugged.

"What?" he asked, biting out the word more than he'd attended.

"I didn't think you'd be here today," Brody drawled. The man hadn't lived in Texas for over a decade, but he liked to pick up the drawl at times. "Thought you said you were going into Montgomery Ink to finish up the piece on your side."

Alex shrugged off his shirt and showed them the freshly done ink, still encased in a wrap. "I can't do much today, but I can at least wrap up my hands and do steady drills on my own."

Harper bent over to look at the ink and whistled. "Austin does amazing work."

"All the Montgomerys do," Brody said. "Though I think I've had at least a partial done from each of the people working at the shop. I just need the new girl, Blake."

Alex rolled his eyes at Brody's tone. "You have a death wish, you know. She's with Maya's brother-in-law, Graham, and you keep trying to flirt with her."

Brody winked. "I only flirt if they flirt back. And I don't actually mean it when I do it. Neither do they."

Alex knew that was true, and why Hailey, Blake, and even Maya laughed and joked with the other man. It was just how Brody was. He'd never once made a woman feel uncomfortable, and there was something to be said for that.

The man was just a nice guy who cared about those in his circle.

Alex wasn't even able to keep the one woman he couldn't get off his mind from running the other direction as soon as he walked into a room.

And that was enough of thinking about *her*.

He rolled his shoulders, doing his best to try and feel out the way his skin stretched along his side. "You guys ready to work out?"

Harper studied his face but didn't say anything while Brody just nodded. The three of them had met off and on around town before they'd shown up on the same day at the gym for boxing lessons. Now, they worked out together and boxed, fought, and learned new techniques any time they could each get away. All of them were single, and were in the middle of new changes in their lives, so coming together to beat the shit out of each other had made them a different kind of friends, but Alex didn't mind it.

They hadn't known the man Alex was before rehab, so they hadn't seen him at his worst.

They only saw him bruised, bloody, and sweaty now after trying to work out his demons the only way he could.

He couldn't drink to bury them anymore.

He might as well try to beat the shit out of them.

****

Tabby was running late, and it was no fault of her own. Even knowing that, she was still frazzled. The phone hadn't stopped ringing since she'd shown up that morning, and she was about to throw it against the wall. There had been a pipe issue at one of the job sites so Wes had been out of the office the entire day dealing with that. Storm had been in a meeting with an upcoming client that had only been scheduled for two hours but had taken seven because the client kept wanting to add things that would affect the structural integrity of the house. Storm had to rush off to another meeting onsite right after, and Tabby didn't even have time to talk to him before he'd left her alone in the building.

Decker, Luc, and Meghan had been onsite all day, as well, dealing with issue after issue, and while that wasn't unusual, it had put more work on her shoulders when someone came in to speak to them. She didn't get how people didn't understand that they needed to call in first to see if someone were actually in the building before showing up with a hundred different questions. But she dealt with it anyway.

Now it was almost five o'clock, and while she usually worked until after six, she'd wanted to go home on time today since she had a roast in the crockpot. She also had it on her planner to call her mother that night, and those calls usually took upwards of two hours.

Her head actually hurt just thinking about how much she had to do, but she'd do it, and if anyone were watching, she'd do it with a smile on her face.

Damn it.

The phone rang yet again, and she hummed to herself, wondering if anyone would notice if she let it go to voicemail. She was alone in the building, after all. But that wasn't Tabby, and she just needed to deal with it for another hour, if not less.

She rolled her shoulders and let out a breath before answering the phone once again. This was what she lived for, usually. Putting pieces together and organizing things until they worked was what she did and what she was darn good at.

"Hello, Montgomery Inc., this is Tabby, how may I help you?"

The door to the building opened as the other person on the line spoke, and she turned to watch Alexander walk in. He brushed snow off his shoulders and looked around the mostly empty room until his gaze settled on her.

She licked her lips, annoyed with herself once again for staring like a teenage lust addict.

"Hello?"

She blinked as Alexander tilted his head toward her and moved closer. Though it wasn't merely walking or moving, he prowled. She wasn't even sure he was aware he did it.

"Sorry, yes, we can schedule that." She nodded as she wrote down a message and added the time to her computer calendar before hanging up. "Alexander, I didn't know you would be in today."

He shrugged off his coat and set down his computer bag. "I was at Decker's site for most of the day, taking photos of the men and women working and getting some behind the scenes shots. I thought I'd come by here and get some pics of people working before the end of the day, but I didn't realize you'd be the only one here."

He shuffled from foot to foot, and she swallowed hard. "Is it a problem I'm the only one here?" Did he not want to be alone with her? And why did that matter anyway?

She was giving herself a headache, and frankly, she needed to get a grip.

He shook his head. "No, I was just surprised. That's all. Are you usually here by yourself when it's dark out?"

She frowned. "It's only just now getting dark, and since we're headed toward spring, it's going to stay light for longer and longer as the days progress. And I'm perfectly fine on my own. Your brothers put up security for the whole building."

He held up his hands in surrender. "Sorry. I just worry about my sisters, and I guess I didn't like the fact that you're here alone when it's dark out, and snow is on the ground."

She ground her back molars. "I'm not your sister."

His eyes darkened, or maybe she just imagined it. A trick of the light maybe. "I know."

She licked her lips. "Good, then." The phone rang. "I have to answer this."

"Go ahead. I'm going to take a few shots around and see what comes to me. Do you mind?"

She waved him off as she answered the phone yet again, doing her best to ignore him and the way his muscles bulged as he pulled his camera out of its case. Damn the man for being so attractive.

And damn her for not only staring but liking the man beneath, as well.

She took notes once again as the person on the other line relayed their problem, and she tried not to look at Alexander as he snapped photos of empty desks and worktables. When he turned to her with his camera in hand, she froze, her phone at her ear.

He pulled his face away from his camera and looked at her before she ducked her head, embarrassed to have caught him snapping a photo of her. She'd known he would be taking photos of everyone who worked at Montgomery Inc., but she hadn't really thought about what that would mean for her.

She finished up the phone call as he packed up his bag. "Are you done, then?"

He nodded. "I'm still getting the feel of what the project's going to look like."

She shook her head at that. "I'm such a planner that I'd probably have four notebooks already with an outline of what I needed to do."

"My brain doesn't work like that, unfortunately. I wish it did since it would probably make my job a bit easier. But with things like this, I can only have a vague idea of what I need until it snaps into place for me."

"Well, if you ever need an extra notebook if you want to try planning, I have a few dozen." She closed her mouth as her eyes widened, and she felt her cheeks heat. She hadn't meant to let him know about that little nugget of her nerdiness.

"Only a few dozen?" he asked with a grin. "You sound like Wes."

She shrugged. "There's a reason he hired me."

Alexander studied her face. "I can see that."

They looked at one another for a few more moments without speaking, and she wasn't sure what to say or what was going on. There was...something. Or perhaps she just imagined it.

"Are you almost done here for the day?"

She forced herself out of her odd thoughts and nodded. "Yes, actually. I might have a few things to do at home, but business hours are done."

He shrugged his coat back on. "I'm going to go scrape off your car if that's okay with you."

"You don't have to do that."

He leveled her a look. "No, but I want to. And I'll be out there anyway doing mine. That way, you won't be out in the parking lot in the dark."

"There are street lights, you know," she said dryly.

"Just let me." He held out his hands. "Please. And if you give me your keys, I'll get your car warmed up, too."

She let out a sigh. She had three older brothers and had been working long enough with the Montgomerys to know when to just give in and let the guy act all caveman. She quickly got her keys out of her purse and handed them to him.

"Do you know which one it is?" They shared a parking lot with a few buildings so she knew there couldn't be just the two vehicles out there.

"Yep. I've known you for a while now, Tabitha. Even if it doesn't seem like it."

She met his gaze, knowing there was something else going on she couldn't quite place. "Thank you." She cleared her throat. "For my car."

He nodded in answer and left her alone to pack up. She let out a breath as soon as he'd left and got to work. She just had one more thing she had to do, and then she'd be ready to go. Honestly, she couldn't just leave him out there in the cold all alone for too long.

She had her back to the door when it opened again. "You were fast," she said as she turned, only to see it wasn't Alexander.

No, this was a larger man with big arms and a bigger gut whom she recognized as one of their former clients. She kept a pleasant look on her face, though her body was on alert. She didn't know why this guy was here, and she had a feeling this wasn't going to end well.

"How can I help you?" she asked, her voice surprisingly calm.

"You already helped enough, bitch. Did you think I'd just pay your fucking fees and be done with it? You Montgomerys are all a bunch of crooks. Liars and cheats. I'm not paying that bill damn it. Fuck you."

She reached out for the phone though she kept her eyes on him. "I'm sorry you're not happy with your bill."

He moved then, and she tried to get away, but he was faster. His hands dug into her arms, and he slammed her back into the wall. Her head snapped back, and she bit her tongue hard enough to taste blood. Fear poured through her, and her pulse raced. This guy was just so freaking big.

She couldn't fight back.

She was helpless.

How...how could she be helpless?

The guy got closer to her face and squeezed her arms. "Fuck. You."

She kicked at him, and he slapped her hard across the face. Tears slid down her cheeks, and she tried to fight back, but she wasn't strong enough.

Before the guy could hit her again, someone pulled him off her.

She fell to the ground on her butt, gasping for breath as she tried to calm her tears and figure out what was going on. Alexander was on top of the other man, hitting him over and over in the face until she was afraid the guy who had attacked her—Charles, yes, that was his name—was dead.

Tears still sliding down her cheeks, she stood on shaky legs and made her way to Alexander's side.

"Stop," she breathed. "Stop," she said again, this time stronger as she put her hand on his shoulder.

Alexander lowered his arm and looked over at her, his eyes wild. "Are you okay?"

She was numb so she didn't know, and she told him so.

He let out a curse and stood up over Charles, who she could tell was still breathing but had passed out. "Call the cops. I'll make sure this ass doesn't wake up."

She nodded, aware that they were close to one another but not touching. She needed...she didn't know what she needed.

Tabby pressed her lips together and tried to move. Only she couldn't.

"Oh, hell," Alexander said under his breath and wrapped his arms around her. Unlike when Charles had touched her, she didn't feel fear.

She didn't know what she felt.

He brought her to his chest and ran a hand down her back, whispering to her. "I'm sorry I didn't come in sooner. So fucking sorry." He kept her in his arms as he called the police and told them what had happened. When he'd hung up with them, assured they were on their way, he wrapped both arms around her.

She cried in his hold and tried to stop herself. "I'm sorry. I hate not being in control."

He let out a rough breath. "I know the feeling."

Of course, he did. "I'm sorry."

"Fuck, *I'm* sorry. Don't be sorry, Tabitha." He blew out a breath. "Okay, this is what we're going to do. Once you're healed and feeling better, I'm going to show you how to be in control, okay? I'm going to show you how to protect yourself. Because there's no fucking way I'm going to let this happen to you again, damn it."

She leaned back in his hold even as the police came through the door. "You promise?"

Alexander reached out as if to cup her face before lowering his hand. "I promise."

And for some reason, that promise meant more than anything.

CHAPTER FOUR

Alex closed his eyes, forcing himself to calm down. Only when he tried to do that, he realized this was a dream and he couldn't do anything but watch...couldn't do anything but be too late.

Everything moved slowly here, yet he moved even slower, as if trapped in a familiar fog—the same fog that had taken years from him because he hadn't been strong enough to save himself.

Now, he wouldn't be strong enough to save *her*.

Tabitha kicked and screamed at the man who had her by the throat against the wall, and yet Alex couldn't move fast enough. He couldn't hear their words, only the screaming, and yet he knew if he didn't try to get to her, it would all be too late.

In that moment, Tabitha turned to him, her bright eyes wide with panic and accusation.

"Help me."

He saw her lips move to form the words, yet he couldn't hear them, not over the sound of his own screaming. And he hadn't even known he was making a sound.

He reached for her, but the sound of their shouts turned into a longer, louder buzz that woke him up. With a groan, Alex turned over and hit the button on his phone that also acted as his alarm.

He didn't want to get started for the day, not with the shit dreams he'd had all night, but lying down in bed where all he had were his thoughts to comfort him didn't make him feel any better.

With a sigh, Alex pulled himself to his feet and shuffled naked to the bathroom. After a long evening of speaking with cops and making sure Tabitha was okay, he'd stripped off his clothes at the foot of his bed and had fallen face-first into sleep, naked and emotionally wrung out. His unconsciousness hadn't lasted for long.

Dreams had assaulted him, mirroring the day before as well as morphing into what had happened over a year ago. Glass shattering. Screams. Accusations. Tears. Utter horror. Despair.

And Alex in the middle of it all, bleeding on the floor and helpless when it came to others.

Wes and Storm had shown up at the office soon after Alex had called them, worry and stress evident in their features. He also thought he'd seen confusion and perhaps accusation in their eyes, but he couldn't be sure. That could always be the demons talking once again, and Alex would be damned if he'd allow that to push him over the edge like before.

The twins had been there to see what had happened and had ensured that Tabitha got home safely after being checked out by the EMTs. She hadn't gone to the hospital. Had instead pushed to go home. Alex wasn't sure that had been the right move, but he hadn't been able to speak much once his brothers had shown up.

He wasn't sure what he'd have said anyway.

Tabitha hadn't said a word to him, but he knew he'd see her today. She'd wanted to learn to protect herself right away, and the idiot that he was had agreed to meet her at his gym that afternoon.

He'd seen the red marks on her face that he thought might turn to bruises, and damn if the sight of them didn't make him want to punch something. Thankfully, he'd be at the gym later, but he didn't know if that was soon enough.

His body was riding an edge he couldn't slip, and there was only so many ways he could calm himself. Resigned, he turned on the shower and slid in, wrapping his hand around his cock as he did so. He squeezed his shaft hard, just on the edge of pain.

He groaned, images of Tabitha coming to mind, and he was just enough of an asshole not to push them out of his thoughts. Instead, he imagined her on her knees as she sucked his balls, using her fingers to play with his prostate before licking up his dick and scraping her teeth along the crown.

He imagined his hand fisted in her hair as he slowly slid his cock between her plump lips. She would moan for him and whisper, "Alexander" as he pulled out to tease her.

Alex groaned, and using soap as well as the rushing water to fist himself, he increased his pace. He was already so close, and though he'd decided to rub one off to take that particular edge off, he also wanted to let this image linger.

He swallowed hard as dream-Tabitha rose in his mind. This way, he could capture her mouth with his and save her knees from kneeling too long. He didn't want to hurt her. He only wanted to make her come.

To make *him* come.

Alex squeezed the base of his dick as he imagined taking Tabitha's nipples into his mouth. He'd spent far too long thinking about her nipples. Would they be dark? Brown and luscious. Or maybe a pale pink he could lave with his tongue. Perhaps they'd darken to a ruby red after he'd sucked on them for hours.

Because he felt like even more of a lecher, he forced her image from his mind and pumped himself harder. Yet even as he came, he knew it was because of *her.*

He quickly finished his shower, aware he'd crossed a line once again, and not sure what he could do about it. After he'd dressed, he went to make himself some coffee, though he wouldn't be leaving the house soon. He'd taken enough initial shots of his family working that he figured he could at least start to process some of them and work with what he had as he formulated an idea about the scope of the project. He also had a few other work things he had to attend to since his family wasn't his only job at the moment. While before he might have been freaking out at having to juggle so many balls, he was just damn thankful he had the opportunity to do what he loved and had once been damn good at.

He also had an upcoming project that wasn't on the books yet, but he'd been toying with the idea for a while now. Ever since he'd gotten out of rehab and had wondered what his next step would be, this idea had been tugging on his mind. He didn't know what he'd do with it once he was done, but he could at least get started on it. Any form of inspiration and need that didn't have to do with drinking and addiction had to be better than where he'd started.

At least, that's what he told himself.

He worked for a few hours, editing images and seeing how they could come together to tell a story. He wasn't just taking pictures; he was narrating a thread that was already there just waiting to come out into the light. Sometimes, it was easier than others as the object in his lens was usually the one telling him what came next, but he didn't mind. This was what he loved, and he was damned glad to be back at it.

When his alarm sounded again, he frowned, pulling himself from his thoughts. He'd forgotten he'd set his phone to tell him that he should head down to the gym. It had been a long time since his work had taken him into his mind like that, and damn how he'd missed the feeling.

He stretched his back as he stood, aware he'd been sitting for too long. Maybe he'd get one of those standing desks his brother, Griffin, had. Hell, the man even had a treadmill desk that Autumn had scored for him. Most of his family members worked with their hands enough and moved around enough that it didn't matter if they sometimes had to sit to work. But he and Griffin had more sedentary jobs. Thankfully, Alex needed to move around to actually shoot the photos, but long days in the editing chair were going to kill his back.

That was just one more reason he worked out and fought as hard as he did.

He quickly packed up his bag and headed to the gym, trying to come up with a plan for how to help Tabitha. He didn't know what he was doing, honestly, and now that he thought about it, he knew this was a fucking crazy plan. Just because he'd been formally trained to fight at one point and could take care of himself didn't mean he could teach Tabitha how to do it.

He just hated to think she had *nothing* up her sleeve.

He could still imagine the way she'd tried to fight back and kick out but had been powerless against the much larger man. The brute who might be in jail for now, but would most likely be out on bail soon with a shiny new restraining order in his name.

Since Alex had fisted his hands on the steering wheel, he forced thoughts of the man from his mind. It didn't do him any good right now where he had nowhere to let go of this rage. That was how he'd fallen into the bottle in the first place. Instead, he thought of Tabitha and wanted to curse himself once more.

He pulled up to the gym, oddly revved and on the verge of a breakdown at the same time. How was he supposed to help her when he could barely help himself? He'd started boxing and fighting because it had kept him focused on what he put into his body, and later, he'd had the additional fun of kicking ass in the ring.

Alex rolled his shoulders, grabbed his bag, and headed into the small gym that had been his refuge for the past year. He was still learning how to be a Montgomery again and blend into his family so he could actually feel useful, but for some reason, he felt that connection in this small, stone building that smelled of sweat and looked as if it needed a few coats of paint.

The guys he worked out with here weren't his family by blood, but they'd taken him in and hadn't asked too many questions. Harper and Brody had become another support system, and he knew he could never replace them. The Montgomerys might be his family in truth, but they'd known him before the booze and during. He'd wanted a clean slate with at least one person in his life, and Brody and Harper had filled that spot.

Tabitha would be there soon, and he'd have to figure out how to help her. Since she was probably going to be sore as hell from the night before, he'd probably just show her how to stand and talk to her about what they would do next. He didn't want to overwhelm her.

Hell, he didn't want to overwhelm himself.

Harper and Brody were both in the gym working out with jump ropes near the ring when Alex walked in. Harper set his things down first and frowned.

"I heard about what happened. Everything okay? Tabby wasn't at work today since Wes told her if she showed up he'd carry her out over his shoulder himself."

Alex didn't like the odd tug in his gut at that thought. There was no reason to be jealous of Wes since Alex had nothing to do with Tabitha like that. Wes and Storm were the ones his parents wanted for Tabitha, and hell, either of them would be better for her anyway. She could also do the unthinkable and *not* be with a Montgomery.

"She's on her way here," Alex said with a frown. "I haven't seen her all day, but I told her I'd help teach her how to defend herself."

Brody's brows rose. "You need help with that?"

Alex shook his head. "I think I'll be okay, but just in case, you guys going to be around for the rest of the evening?"

Harper nodded. "Brody wanted to spar so we'll be in the ring for a bit."

Alex relaxed a bit. He'd been afraid he'd be all alone with Tabitha and end up fucking things up. At least he'd have a buffer here.

Brody's eyes darted over Alex's shoulder, and they darkened with rage. "I hope you beat the shit out of that fucker."

Alex turned on his heel as Tabitha hesitantly walked into the gym, her eyes wide as she seemed to take everything in. He probably should have taken her to a nicer place or even the gym his brother-in-law, Decker, had built in his basement, but he'd said the first thing that had come to mind when he'd seen her shaking as he had. He might regret being this close to her when he was still trying to figure out who he was, but he'd be damned if he saw that look in her eyes ever again.

"You're here," he growled low. For some reason, he thought she might have changed her mind and stayed away. He didn't want to think about the feelings inside him that wanted her there right then. The ones that wanted her by his side. Wanted her *with* him.

He paused to clear his throat before moving toward her. The bruises on her face were a stark shadow against the creamy paleness of her skin. His hands fisted at his sides, and he forced himself to loosen them as he studied her face.

She hadn't bothered with makeup that day, or at least for the evening—meaning she hadn't hidden the bruises from him. He didn't know why that pleased him, and he couldn't afford to worry about that right then. She'd left her hair in that ponytail she loved—the same one he'd imagined wrapping around his fist— and it kept the long mass away from her face. That only made the blues and blacks on her face, the evidence of that bastard's hand on her soft skin, stand out.

She wore a thick hoodie over her workout gear, and had a small bag slung over her shoulder. If it weren't for the vivid fear in her eyes and the palpable tension in her shoulders, he'd have figured she was ready to go. It seemed that they were both off their footing a bit here, and he was just going to have to figure out what to do about it.

"I'm here," she finally said after a moment. She gave the place a quick study before raising her brow at him. "I know you said this was a gym, but I didn't quite picture this."

He frowned. "People work out here. It's a gym." It wasn't as steel and mirror-covered as some, and didn't have peppy music and people in bright spandex, but it was a gym. His gym.

She pointed over at one of the boxing rings in the center of the room. "You do more than work out. But since that's why I'm here, I can hardly complain. And I wouldn't be complaining anyway."

She paused, shifting from foot to foot.

He moved closer, aware Harper and Brody were behind him and hadn't said anything. They were most likely listening in on every word and had their eyes on the two of them, but he ignored them for now. This was all about Tabitha.

Alex did something next he knew he might regret, but he did it anyway.

He cupped her cheek, being very cautious of the slight bruising on that side of her face. She had more on the other side, and all he wanted to do was kiss them away.

So he didn't.

"What is it?" he asked, his voice low.

Her eyes widened at his touch, and her lips parted as she let out a gasping breath, her chest rising and falling in the motion.

"Thank you."

He frowned. "For what?"

She narrowed her eyes, and he'd never been so eager to see that spark of temper. That meant she hadn't lost any of her fight. She just needed to fortify it.

"For before and for now. Don't pretend like you don't know."

She stepped back, and whatever moment they'd been having broke. Alex wasn't exactly sorry about that either. Nor was he too relieved.

Hell, this woman confused him, and he wasn't sure he could afford to be confused right now.

"Hi, Harper," Tabitha said as she leaned around Alex. "And it's Brody, right? I saw you at the shop with Austin."

Did Tabitha have a tattoo somewhere? And why was he spending so much time thinking about that?

The guys chatted with her a bit as he gathered his thoughts. He needed to get his head in the game if he were going to accomplish what he'd set out to do and actually help Tabitha take care of herself.

"You ready to go?" he asked, and she turned to face him. Nervousness slid over her features, and he swore to himself that he'd do his best to never see that again on her face. "We can go back to a room over there if you want privacy." He paused, thinking over his word choice when she gave him a curious look. "Unless you'd rather not be alone with me." There were thousands of reasons for her not to be alone with him. The fact that he couldn't stop thinking about her was only one of them.

She shook her head. "I trust you. I wouldn't be here if I didn't."

He swallowed hard at the truth in her gaze.

She trusted him.

If only he trusted himself.

****

"Keep your arms up a little higher."

Tabby shifted in front of Alexander, all too aware of how *big* he seemed. How...*everything*. She was all too aware of him in general these days, and she didn't feel like she could hold herself back as well as she had before. She'd known from the first time she'd walked into the small gym that seemed to hold a piece of him that this whole thing might have been a mistake.

But she'd been so freaking scared about what had happened at the office, and she'd latched on to what she could. Even being here for twenty minutes while Alexander spoke to her made her feel better. Safer.

She may not ever be able to fight like he apparently could, but she'd at least be able to help herself a bit more.

"Okay, don't hold your thumb like that. You'll end up breaking it." He put his large hand over hers, and she forced herself to not suck in a breath at the heat of his touch. With each correction, each graze of flesh, she couldn't help but want him.

Yes, she was here for a reason, but in the humid room with only the two of them there to sweat, touch, and move closer, her brain couldn't help but *imagine*. She could glimpse part of his ink as his shirt shifted, and she wanted to see all of it, wanted to taste it.

She'd been freaking *attacked* last night, and yet she couldn't help but watch Alexander move.

"Got it," she breathed and looked up. She hadn't realized he was so close. All she had to do was go to her tiptoes, and she could brush her lips along his. His gaze dropped to her mouth, and she watched as his Adam's apple bobbed when he swallowed. His tongue darted out to lick his bottom lip, and her nipples became hard points against her sports bra.

His chest moved quicker as his breaths increased, and she ached for him.

But she couldn't move forward, not now. Maybe not ever. He wasn't ready. *She* wasn't ready.

They each took a step back at the same time, and she refused to feel hurt by that. After all, she'd moved, too.

Alexander cleared his throat. "I think that's it for now. You need to rest."

She'd have bristled at the order if she didn't agree with him. "Thank you for at least starting. Can we do it again?" She could have kicked herself for asking. She could take a class if she truly wanted to continue, and while she *did* want to learn more, she wanted *Alexander* to teach her.

She was a glutton for punishment, and yet she couldn't move away.

He studied her face for a moment before giving her a nod. "We can. I just want you safe."

She tried not to look too hard into those words, but she couldn't help it. When it came to him, she couldn't help much.

With one last look, she said her goodbyes as she packed up and hurried to her car, aware that her knees were shaking. While she should go home and shower, she headed to her favorite bookstore instead. Her friend owned and operated the place, and since she couldn't think clearly at the moment, she needed Everly's help to focus.

All of her other friends had married into the Montgomerys, and this was one thing she couldn't talk to them about.

As soon as she'd pulled into the parking lot, she cursed herself. She hadn't bothered to put on concealer before she'd left the house because Alexander had already seen the worst of it. But going into Everly's shop was something different altogether. She couldn't take the pitying looks. Thankfully, it was near the close of business, so hopefully Tabby would be able to sneak right in.

Beneath the Cover was a small indie bookshop that catered to every genre, but half of it was devoted to romance. It was seriously Tabby's favorite store ever. And since it was located in downtown Denver, it had tons of walk-in shoppers, and it was close enough to their friend Hailey's café that they ended up doing promotions together. Somehow, they'd ended up creating a small town feeling inside a huge downtown city.

It made Tabby miss home just a bit less.

Everly was at the cash register, looking over a book when Tabby walked in. Her friend's eyes widened when she saw Tabby, and she hurried around to the front of the shop.

"Oh my God, Tabby. That selfie you sent didn't do this justice. I want to kick that guy's ass so hard right now. Thankfully, Alex did it for me."

Tabby's eyes filled, and she did her best to try and blink the tears away. She fought to keep from crying because, damn it, she'd already cried enough. She wanted to fight back now, and tears would only get in the way.

"It'll heal. *I'll* heal."

"I know you will, honey. Now let me close up shop and we can have some tea before I need to head out and pick up the kids." Everly had two children she raised on her own, and Tabby still didn't know how the other woman did it every day.

"Tea sounds great." Tabby moved to the side as her friend locked the door. "I almost kissed him," she blurted.

Everly turned on her heel, her eyes wide. Her friend knew about Tabby's crush and was the only one who did, but that still didn't make Tabby's words any less awkward.

"If I didn't have to drive, I'd say we need more than tea right now," Everly said slowly. "How close was almost?" she said with a small smile.

Tabby laughed then, just a little bit of her tension leaving her shoulders. "Close enough." She let out a breath. "I don't know what I'm going to do, Ev."

"Then we'll figure it out."

And, apparently, it needed to be as simple as that. But Tabby knew more than most that nothing was ever simple with a Montgomery—Alexander even more so.

CHAPTER FIVE

Alex was fucking this up. Again. He couldn't quite believe he'd been that stupid but considering his past decisions, he couldn't even blame himself.

A strong wind slapped at him, forcing him out of his cyclical thoughts. The cold bit into his skin, but he did his best to ignore it. He couldn't move at that exact moment to shift his scarf to protect his neck and the lower part of his face from the bitter wind. Instead, he let the cold seep into his skin and chill him down to his bones as he focused on his subject.

Hand on the lens, he changed what he needed to before pressing the shutter.

Click.

Another angle.

Click.

This one more focused.

Click.

Move, one more time.

Click.

Let out a breath.

Click.

Alex lowered the camera and blinked away the intense haze that always came from shooting a subject. His brain had been focused not only on the one man in front of him but also the thousand different parts of the setting that worked around both of them in the downtown Denver area.

"Got what you need?" the man in front of him growled out. "Don't know why you want to take a picture of me just sitting here, but if that gets your rocks off, go for it." The homeless man patted his torn jacket and gave Alex a yellow-stained smile. "I got my sandwich so I guess that's all I need." He narrowed his eyes. "Unless you got a few bucks you can spare."

Alex shook his head. "Sorry. All out. I do have coffee for you if you want."

The older man snorted. At least Alex thought the man was older than he was, but for all he knew, the booze had just made the homeless guy in front of him appear aged.

"No. Can't stand the stuff. Bad for my indigestion." Alex nodded his thanks for helping him but figured the other man didn't want it. And he had a feeling it wasn't coffee that hurt the man's stomach, but the lack of booze in his system. There was a reason Alex didn't give the homeless people around money anymore. He'd seen what happened after he'd done that a few times when he came back the next day. Not everyone would spend their money on alcohol or drugs or even cigarettes, but enough had done it that Alex had learned his lesson.

He'd also learned that not everyone was truly homeless. He'd been burned a few times from supposedly homeless men or women or even *kids* who panhandled before jumping on their thousand dollar bike or even getting inside their Mercedes parked a couple of blocks away.

He might have done his best to not judge, but those people pissed him off more than anything.

So instead of waiting to see how those he tried to help spent their money, he paid people in food, coffee, and blankets. He usually ended up giving people stuff like that regardless if they helped him out on his project, but those who *did* help, got more out of him. He knew it wasn't enough, wasn't *nearly* enough, but this small thing was all he could do for now. Maybe one day he'd be in a position to do even more.

Alex walked down the darkened streets of downtown Denver and tried to see the area from each perspective. He took photos when he felt the urge and did his best to come up with a story for each setting.

The city had a homeless problem, but hell, so did many major cities. The problem with Denver was that since it was located out west, there weren't as many major cities for people to travel around to. The metro areas out east were closer together, and because of that, the nomadic nature of many of the homeless was easier. Not that anything was easy, but it was still easier than being out west where there weren't many—if any—other cities around.

During the day, people in suits and fancy clothes would drive by in their fancier cars to park at their high-rises. Others took the bus or light rail and commuted into the city from their suburban homes. There was a younger population within the city, as well; those who wanted to live in those high-rises or apartments that were way too expensive for Alex's tastes. There was even a major University settled downtown that shared a campus with a community and smaller college.

There were hundreds of people in all different shapes, sizes, and economic means that passed him every day. And each of those people also passed the men and women unconscious on the street corners from either too little food or too many drinks.

The city was a mix of everything, and Alex wanted to catch a glimpse of it.

That's why his latest project centered on what he could have become if he hadn't had his family by his side. He'd almost pushed them all away to the point he could have lost it all, but they hadn't let him. They'd held on to him even as he'd tried to buck them off, and in the end, he'd needed them far more than he'd even thought possible. Without them, he'd have lost himself. Without them, he could have become one of the people he passed as he walked down 16th Street Mall.

Or maybe he would have drunk himself to death long before that.

He didn't know what he would have become if he hadn't gone to rehab, but he'd be damned if he'd become anything close to that man again. He was different now. Or at least the shell coating him was. Inside, he wasn't sure anymore. Without the alcohol to drown out the demons, he knew they were there, taunting him. But over time, he prayed they would quiet down, and he'd find the strength to become some semblance of the man he'd once been.

He let out another breath as a gust of wind slapped at him. It was too damn cold for anyone to be out as they were, but the shelters were closing soon for the evening, and there wasn't enough room for everyone. Alex figured he had another ten minutes in him to try and take a few more photos before he needed to get in his car and head home. He couldn't risk getting sick and getting behind in his work. This project didn't have a backer yet, and he wasn't sure what he was going to do with it, but he just *knew* he had to finish it. Meaning those projects that he *was* hired for had to be a priority so he could have things like heat in his home and food in his belly.

He'd lost the house in the divorce, but he'd been fine with that in the end. He might not have cared too much when he'd been drinking, but now that he was out of that haze, he knew he could never have slept there again anyway. Instead of the sprawling ranch-style house he'd tried to make into a home with his ex-wife, he'd rented a small two-bedroom apartment in a decent suburb. He'd turned one of the rooms into a darkroom, though he rarely worked outside of digital anymore. The dining area had been made into his office, and somehow, he'd made it all work.

At least, he hoped he had.

With his hands in his pockets, he turned down one of the streets off the Mall and took a look around. He'd been down this road countless times before and knew it like the back of his hand. This was the place his family had made, the world they'd created. The tattoo shop, Montgomery Ink, lay on one side of the street. Across from that, his sister-in-law's place, Eden, stood, bright and ready for customers, though he figured it would be closing for the evening soon. Next to the tattoo shop was Taboo, Hailey's café. Hailey was a family friend, though he figured she knew him the least out of all the Montgomerys.

His fault, of course.

Near the café was a bookshop he'd never been in, but his family had, and he figured he should stop in eventually to see if his brother Griffin had a few books in stock. Alex always liked to pick up one or two, even though he had them all. He made sure to leave a few on the shelves though so others could pick them up and get addicted to the series like Alex was.

Every single one of his siblings was so freaking talented.

He just hoped he could find the talent he'd once held in his hands again.

His phone buzzed in his pocket as he headed to where he'd parked his car behind the tattoo shop, and he slid off his gloves to take it out. He cursed at the cold and told himself he'd buy some of those high-tech gloves that could sense heat or whatever so he didn't have to take them off to use his smartphone.

"What's up, Storm?" Alex asked as he hunched down low. It was getting colder by the minute, and he wanted inside his damn car. He hadn't meant to stay out this long, but he'd found four different people who'd wanted their story told. So he'd taken notes and photos and promised them he'd do something with them that meant something. What it was, he didn't know yet.

"Why do you sound out of breath?" Storm asked.

"Because it's colder than Frosty's balls right now."

Storm let out a chuckle. "I didn't know Frosty had balls. And, hell, how do you know how cold they are?"

"You can't see me, but I'm flipping you off." Not really since there were still people out on the streets and he didn't want to be *that* guy, but his brother would get the idea.

"Fuck you, too." Storm snorted. "What are you doing outside if it's so cold?"

He hadn't told anyone about his project yet since he didn't have a name for it, and honestly, it was a little more personal than he'd thought it would be. "I'm headed to my car. What do you want?"

"Well, I was going to see if you wanted to get dinner, but if you're going to be an asshole, I change my mind."

Alex's stomach rumbled, but he shook his head. Then he remembered his brother couldn't see him. Hell, the cold had taken his brain cells along with his warmth, apparently. "Can we do it tomorrow?" He didn't have plans for dinner, but he wanted to refine his notes tonight while they were still fresh in his mind.

"No problem." Storm paused. "Glad you want to."

He let the sting slap at him as was its due. He'd said "no" to more dinners with his family than he should have in the past, and he'd be damned if he did that again.

A flash of red caught his eye and he froze.

Auburn red hair that he dreamed about.

"What the fuck?"

"What? What's wrong?" Storm asked, his voice intent.

"I thought I just saw...never mind." Alex shook his head again. "I gotta go. See you tomorrow for dinner."

"What the hell, Alex?"

He ended the call as his brother questioned him, knowing he'd get hell for it later. But first, Alex had to follow that flash of red. He picked up his pace to almost a jog and turned down a darkened alley, his senses on alert.

There she was in her prim jacket and scarf, a bag in her hand and worry on her face. He'd have thought she looked fucking beautiful even with the red cheeks and nose, but he couldn't quite think that hard right then, not with the rage in his system.

"What the fuck are you doing here in the dark?" he bit out.

Tabitha's eyes widened as her gaze met his. "Alexander."

He went straight to her, knowing he probably looked like a crazy man right then. He didn't care. "What. The. Fuck."

****

Shit. What was Alexander doing here? Of all the Montgomerys she might have seen near the Mall area, Alexander was the last on her list of people she wanted to see. Damn it. She hadn't wanted him to see her like this. He saw too much, asked too many questions. She wasn't ready to share what she was doing or *why* she was doing it.

Only, for some reason, she knew she couldn't hide it from the man currently growling in front of her.

"What. The. Fuck."

"What do you mean?" she finally said, her throat dry. "I'm walking."

He looked at her as if she'd lost a few brain cells, and perhaps she had, as this wasn't the first time she'd done this. But, frankly, it wouldn't be the last.

"You're walking. In a dark alley. Alone. At night. In a bright white coat that screams for someone to attack you. What the fuck, Tabitha?"

She narrowed her eyes. "Will you stop saying that?"

"No. I'm not going to stop asking what the fuck until you tell me what the fuck."

"It's none of your business." And it wasn't. "I have pepper spray and my whistle."

He rolled his eyes. "Good for you. And since I've given you, what, *one* lesson in self-defense, you must but all ready to take care of yourself in a dark alley." He reached out as if to touch the fading bruises on her face before thinking better of it and dropping his hand to her elbow. The sensation of his hand on her, even through the thickness of her coat was enough to take her breath away.

She let out a shaky breath. "Stop treating me like I'm stupid."

"Then stop acting stupid," he bit out.

She ignored the sting of his words and tried to move past him. *They* weren't here anyway. Once again, her trek out here was another lost cause. She should be used to it by now.

Alexander gripped her elbow harder, and she froze. "What are you doing out here?" He'd lowered his voice to a decibel that meant it slid over her like smooth velvet. Damn the man.

"None of your business. What are *you* doing out here?"

He frowned and lifted his camera. "Working."

Surprised he'd answered at all, she blinked at him. "Oh."

"Yeah. Oh. Come on, I'll get you to your car."

She shook her head. "I took the light rail." She always did for this in case she saw them

He pinched the bridge of his nose. "At night. Alone. Hell, Tabitha. Come on, I'll take you home. I parked behind the shop."

She dug her feet into the cement and stood her ground. "You can't drag me off like a caveman. I have rights."

He cursed under his breath. "Yeah, you do. And right now, you're using those *rights* to be an idiot. I'll throw you over my shoulder and carry you out of here if I have to."

She wanted to stomp her foot like a two-year-old but figured that wouldn't help her cause. "Stop calling me stupid and an idiot. I'm not either of those. I came prepared."

Like you were prepared that night in your office? He didn't say it, but she knew he was thinking it.

"Let me take you home." He paused. "Please."

It was the please that did it, and she figured he'd known it would. She let him lead her out of the alley and toward his car. Though he had his hand on her elbow, she knew she wouldn't leave him right then. It hadn't been the smartest idea to come out in this weather, but she'd spent too many days inside because of the attack, and she'd been afraid she'd miss them. Contrary to what Alexander thought, she wasn't an idiot. She carried pepper spray and didn't usually walk down dark alleys.

Usually.

When they got to his car, he held her door open for her and slammed it after she'd gotten in. Apparently, his temper wasn't quite through.

"Did you need to say goodbye to your family?" she asked as he got into his seat.

He shot her a look before turning on the car. "What's your address?"

She blinked and rattled it off as he plugged it into the car's navigation system. She could have just told him where she lived and given him directions, but she wasn't sure he was in the mood for that right then. It also occurred to her that he'd never been to her home. Wes and Storm had in the past to drop things off or even pick them up, but Alexander had never had a reason to come to her place.

Until now.

Of course, now she was wondering if she'd left her laundry basket in the living room or if she'd washed her dishes from earlier. She might be in love with organizing, but mid-cleaning never looked wonderful.

But what did it matter?

He'd probably just drop her off in front of her house and speed away, annoyed that he'd had to stop whatever he was doing to save the poor damsel in distress.

She wasn't a fucking damsel.

"You're going to break a molar if you keep your jaw that tight," Alex bit out as he drove.

She shot him a look. "You're one to talk."

His mouth quirked up in a smile before he frowned again. She loved it when he smiled, but she wished he did it more often. Of course with the way he was acting right now, she really wanted nothing to do with him. Maybe his actions tonight would get the annoying crush out of her system once and for all.

Only she had a feeling it was only going to make it worse. They didn't speak after that, but the tension in the car increased with each passing mile. She didn't know if his came from his anger or what, but *hers* was a mix of everything. She didn't like Alexander too much right then, but damn if she didn't want him. She licked her lips; her breath quickening, and she did her best to ignore how good he looked in profile.

He shot her a look, his eyes darkening under the passing streetlights, and he abruptly turned back to stare at the road. His hands tightened on the steering wheel, and she wondered what on earth he could be thinking right then.

When he pulled into her driveway, she expected him to let her out and leave. Instead, he got out of the car with her and stalked toward her front door by her side. She didn't say a word as she opened the door and took a step inside. She turned on her heel to say goodbye and thank him for walking her to her door; only he pushed past her and slammed the door closed.

"Excuse me," she clipped. "I did *not* invite you into my home. If you're going to be an asshole and judge me for my actions, you can get out right now. I don't have to take it."

"I like seeing the spark in your eyes, babe. That means you're not stupid. But fuck, Tabitha, I still don't know why you were out there."

"And you don't need to know." No one did. "And don't call me 'babe.'"

His eyes darkened even more, and he took a step toward her. She leaned back and ended up pressed against the door, her chest heaving as she fought to catch her breath. He reached out and traced her cheek with his finger, his gaze on hers.

"What am I going to do with you, Tabitha?"

She swallowed hard, unsure what to say. That was probably why she said what she did next. "What do you want to do with me?"

His eyes widened marginally as if she'd surprised him. "Are you sure you want to know?" He lowered his head, and she tilted her chin up ever so slightly.

"Tell me."

Instead of answering, he pressed his forehead to hers. "You scared the shit out of me. Don't do that again."

She closed her eyes. "I can't promise that."

He cursed under his breath. "Then take me with you next time. But don't go out again alone." He paused. "Please."

Once again, it was the please that did it. "Alexander—"

She didn't have time to finish her statement—not that she knew what she was going to say anyway. Alexander crushed his mouth to hers, cupping her chin and forcing her to her tiptoes. She froze for a moment, wondering how the hell they'd ended up here. Then he cupped her breast, and she pushed all thoughts other than having his hands and lips on her out of her mind.

She moaned against him, rocking her body hard along his as he molded her breasts with his hands. As he roamed her body, she reached around to dig her fingers into his back, his ass. Anything she could hold on to.

And this man was all lean muscles so there was a lot of *hard* to hold on to.

He kissed down her neck and tugged on the collar of her jacket. She helped him by quickly stripping it off, the pool of soft fabric landing on the floor by her feet turning her on even more. He quickly did the same to his jacket, and they were back on each other, their hands touching what they could, their lips meeting in heat and breathlessness.

He growled before kissing down her chest and sucking her nipple through her long sweater and bra. She rocked her head back against the door, gripping him to keep herself steady since she knew her knees were about to give out.

"What are we doing?" she gasped, annoyed with herself for even asking the question.

His gaze met hers as he slowly slid his hand up under her sweater dress and over the seam of her leggings. He cupped her boldly, and her mouth went dry once again.

"What do you want to do?"

"*Everything*," she gasped.

"Good." He slid his hand up and over the top of her leggings and then behind her waistband. Before she could take another breath, he had his hand under her panties and his fingers sliding between her almost embarrassingly wet folds.

She closed her eyes, reveling in the sensation.

"Eyes, babe. Let me see your eyes."

She cracked open her lids, her mouth parted. When he inserted a finger, she moaned, her head going back but her eyes never leaving his.

"You're so fucking wet for me, Tabitha. So. Fucking. Wet. I could come right now with just my hand on your pussy. That's how hot you make me.

She rolled her hips on his hand, riding him, and they both groaned.

"That's it, babe. Ride me. Show me how much you want this."

She'd never been into dirty talk with her past lovers because she'd always thought it was silly, but Alexander blew all her previous thoughts out of the window. He rubbed his thumb over her clit, and she came just like that, her inner walls tightening on his finger and her body shaking in his hold.

When she came down from her high, he rested his head on hers, his hand still down her pants. "I don't have a fucking condom. Damn it. It's been—" he cut himself off.

It had been a while for him. That much she knew. He'd been so good over the past year or so because he'd been focused on healing. That was why he didn't carry a condom with him.

"In my bag," she said softly. "I keep one on me."

She blushed as he grinned at her. "What? I want to be prepared and not have to rely on the guy to keep me safe. Got a problem with that?"

He slid his hand out of her pants and licked his fingers. "No problem at all."

She almost came again.

He bent over to retrieve her fallen purse, and she quickly pulled a condom out of the side pocket. She replaced it every few months since it had been a *long* time since she'd been with a man, but she never wanted to be unprepared.

Of course, nothing could have prepared her for Alexander.

He undid his pants and pulled out his length. She only caught a quick glimpse as he rolled the condom over his cock, but she liked what she saw. Before she could fully come back down from her previous high, he pulled down her leggings. Somehow they ended up tangled around one ankle over a boot with the other leg and foot free. He pulled her panties to the side and met her gaze before sliding in to the hilt with one stroke.

She gasped, her body stretching to accommodate his girth as he froze, sweat covering his temples. They still wore most of their clothes, and she hadn't even seen all of him—nor he of her—and yet she knew this had to be the single most erotic moment of her life.

Tabby slid her hands over his shoulders and gripped. "Alexander…" she breathed.

He kissed her lips softly, neither of them closing their eyes as he did. Her heart caught, and she fell for him once more; fell for this man she thought she knew and was only now finding the truth depths of.

Then he moved.

She rocked with him, their lovemaking hard and fast against the door. Each thrust banged the wood hard against its hinges, and she figured anyone outside would be able to hear what was going on, but she didn't care.

All she wanted was to come around Alexander's cock and have him release inside her.

She wanted to *feel*.

She wanted to *be*.

She wanted *Alexander*.

When she came again, he lifted her up so she could wrap her legs around his waist, and he caught her mouth with his.

"You're so fucking beautiful when you come," he growled, his hips still thrusting. "Now I want to see *all* of you."

He pulled out of her, and she already missed him. But before she could miss him too much, he had them both naked, their hands roaming each other. His on her breasts, over her clit, and gripping her ass. Hers on his ass, as well, down his chest, and gripping the base of his cock within the dark hair there.

She squeezed, and he cursed.

"Not until I'm in you," he growled and spun her around to face the back of the couch. She gripped the fabric as he pistoned into her from behind. He had one hand on her hip, keeping her steady, while the other pinched her nipples and slid down her stomach.

"Feel me, Tabitha. I've never felt anything as good as your cunt squeezing me as you come. Can you feel me inside you? Can you feel how hot I am for you?"

She threw her head back. "Fuck me."

He laughed, but it wasn't humor in the sound, it was need. "I am, babe. I am."

When he probed her ass with his fingers, she lost her rhythm. He didn't stop, though; instead, he massaged her, gently probing the edge without actually penetrating her until she came.

She'd already come three times that night. She wasn't sure she would be able to do it again, and he hadn't even come once. When he pulled away, she turned and reached between them.

"No, you touch me, and I'll come." He gripped her wrist and tugged her arm behind her. Then he slid his arm under her ass and lifted her so she sat on the back of the couch.

"That's kind of the idea," she teased, spreading for him.

He licked his lips, swallowing hard. "You're so fucking wet, babe. And as much as I want to come, I want to be *inside* you when I do. So no mouth or hands on my cock tonight. And, yeah, I want to eat you so bad, but not right now. Later."

Would there be a later?

Before she could ask that question or blurt something equally stupid, he rubbed the head of his cock between her swollen folds, keeping his eyes on hers as he slowly, oh so slowly, slid deep inside her. She broke eye contact to look between them where they were joined, the sight so freaking hot she thought she'd break down right there.

"Eyes. Give me your eyes, Tabitha."

She gave him her eyes.

And when they both came together, she kept her eyes on his, knowing she was risking it all because they'd reveal too much. Yet in that instant, she saw something she couldn't place in his gaze.

What did it mean?

What did he want?

And what the *hell* had she just done?

CHAPTER SIX

What the hell had he just done?

Alex had his cock in the one woman he shouldn't have, and he had a feeling he'd bared more than his body just then. No, he'd bared something far worse.

Himself.

He couldn't risk that. He couldn't risk Tabitha by exposing her to what lay beneath his skin.

As carefully as he could, he slowly slid out of her, his cock already hardening again at the sight before him. She was flushed from her orgasms, her nipples that dark red he'd imagined them being. They were even better in person, and he hadn't even had a chance to truly feast on them. He also hadn't had the opportunity to eat the fantastic wet cunt in front of him as he'd also imagined doing because he'd been too busy trying to get inside her.

He'd fucked everything up, and he had no idea how to fix it.

"Alexander?"

Her voice was hesitant as if she were afraid he'd run at too loud of a noise.

Well, she probably had a right to be afraid of that.

"I need to take care of the condom."

She blinked. "There's a bathroom right down the hall."

He nodded before awkwardly patting her hip. He winced at the confused look on her face before quickly picking up his clothes and heading to the bathroom. He threw away the condom and splashed some cold water on his face before pulling his clothes back on.

He hadn't meant to make love to her.

Hell, he hadn't meant to kiss her.

But they had kissed and much more, and now they'd have to deal with it.

His hands shook as that seductive temptress that was his addiction clawed at him.

He needed a drink.

Instead, he shot a text off to his sponsor and let out a breath.

He wasn't good enough for Tabitha, and damn it, they both knew that. This was a mistake. It couldn't be anything more.

He made his way to the living room where she'd thrown on the blanket that had been on the back of the couch before he'd fucked her on top of it.

"I need to go."

The hurt look that slid over her face kicked him in the gut, but he had to ignore it. He *had* to. He wasn't sure he was strong enough to stay.

She seemed to collect herself before nodding. "Okay."

He was an asshole. The worst kind of man. "I'll see you soon." They had to work together, and if she wanted to continue, train together.

"I'm sure you will."

She didn't sound hurt, and that's how he knew he'd hurt her more than he'd thought possible. And yet... he still had to go.

He stepped forward as if to kiss her goodbye and froze. She met his gaze and nodded, and he figured she might understand. That didn't make it right. He turned and left through the front door, closing it softly behind him.

When he got into his car, he gripped the steering wheel hard. He took a deep breath, centering himself as much as he was able. Sweat trickled down his back, and he forced himself to turn on the engine. He pulled out of Tabitha's drive, aware she could be watching him through the window. He wouldn't blame her, though, if she hadn't given him a second thought as soon as he'd walked away. He deserved that. He didn't want to think about the look in her eyes, only he knew he should.

She deserved more than that.

She deserved more than him.

The phone through his Bluetooth buzzed, and he let out a breath as soon as he saw the readout. He answered, his hands barely steady.

"Steve." His sponsor.

"Alex. Tell me what you're thinking." Alex had sent a quick text to the other man, their code for needing help but not fully over the edge yet. They had a few codes.

"I'm not going to drink," he told his sponsor. And himself. "Not today. Not tomorrow."

Steve didn't sigh with relief or tell him good job. He did the only thing Alex needed right then.

"Do you want to meet?"

Alex shook his head, although Steve couldn't see him. "No." He took a deep breath. "No," he repeated, firmer this time. "I just needed a reminder."

"I'm here if and when you need me." A pause. "Want to tell me what happened?"

There were no secrets between him and Steve, at least not on Alex's end. That's the only way he stayed sane.

"I slept with Tabitha."

Steve let out an audible breath, and Alex could only imagine the look on the other man's face. "I knew you'd thought about it, but I hadn't realized it had gotten that far."

Alex's fingers once again tightened on the wheel. "It was...unexpected." That was an understatement. He had been so fucking worried about her, so angry that she could have been in danger again, that he hadn't been able to control his urges when it came to her. And that was what scared him. For the past year, he'd been able to contain his need for her, to hide the fact that he wanted her even if he was only just now getting to know more and more about her. But he'd lost control and had moved too fast.

Or maybe not fast enough.

And because he couldn't think straight, that's why he knew he had to talk to Steve.

And then...and then talk to Tabitha.

"Okay. I'm not going to tell you what to think, only that you need to breathe. You and I both discussed how we thought you were ready to date since you hit the one-year mark. If you aren't ready, after all, we can talk about that, too."

Alex pulled over into an empty parking lot so he could think. "Let's talk, then," he said softly.

"Let's talk."

At home, Alex tried to remember his normal routine, only he couldn't focus. Routines usually helped him work through the worst of the temptations. Right now, though, what he wanted most wasn't a drink, but rather the woman he'd left naked and vulnerable in her living room.

He was truly the worst kind of asshole.

What he needed was to take a shower and go to sleep so he could face the next morning. He didn't know what was coming or how he would get through it, only that he would. He wouldn't fail this time. He refused to.

He showered quickly, his body still thrumming from Tabitha's touch even though he'd already sated himself—or so he'd thought. He could scent her on his skin, in his pores. And yet, no matter how much he knew he should try, he didn't wash it fully away. He didn't scrub until he couldn't smell her anymore because, damn it, he would *always* know her scent now. He would always know her taste, how she felt surrounding his cock, how she looked when she came, how her nipples darkened under his gaze.

He groaned and gripped the base of his cock, annoyed with himself for getting hard all over again.

He didn't deserve her.

Alex turned the shower to cold and blasted his skin, hoping it would take most of the heat away. It only partially worked but even a little had to count for something.

Once he got into bed, he sank into the middle of the mattress, aware he would once again be sleeping alone. But he should have been used to it by now.

He'd been alone far longer than people knew.

He didn't go into the office that day. Though he probably should have, he'd called Wes and said he wanted to try and map out what he had instead of getting more material for the time being. His brother hadn't thought anything of it, but Alex knew he was taking the coward's way out. He just needed a day or so to figure out what he was doing before he saw her again. With Tabitha around, his brain went fuzzy, and he never said the right thing or did what he was supposed to do.

After he'd made himself some coffee, he pulled out his camera and started to work. He hadn't lied to Wes when he'd said he had things to do with what he already had. Of course, he could have always gotten more shots since he still wasn't sure the route he wanted to take with the family project, but he could at least start.

He set aside his work from the night before and put it in a folder on his portable hard drive and the cloud. His mind wasn't quite ready to go down memory lane with that yet because every time he thought about it, he'd think of Tabitha now.

So, of course, the first photo he opened for the Montgomery project was that of Tabitha looking down, her face slightly away from the camera, her fingers tracing her ear as she blushed.

He swallowed hard.

Damn it.

He'd made a mistake. He shouldn't have slept with her. She was so much more than he deserved, and she needed someone better than a drunk who struggled every day with sobriety.

After taking a deep breath, he went back to work. As he looked through the images, a story began to unfold. It wasn't always like that for him, but when it was, he knew to grab on and not let go. There were pictures of Storm bent over his workbench, his complete concentration on his project as if trying to get every angle so perfect that they'd form exactly what the client wanted and what he, himself, needed to see. He had images of Wes working with a hammer and later on his phone as he worked with his tablet and talked to someone at the same time. His brother was always good at multitasking. There were other photos of his brother-in-law, Decker, manning his crew and laughing with his wife when she visited. More of Luc and Meghan working side by side on their own projects, the looks they gave one another private but still out in the open for everyone to see. There were more photos of the crew like Harper and some of the loading guys, laughing as they sweated under the icy sun that was Denver's winter.

Each photo individually told a story about that person and how much they loved their job. But together, it wove a tale of togetherness and hard work. The Montgomerys had built something unique and perfect.

And now, Alex would do his damnedest to show that off for not only the website and packets but also maybe another project that would be just for the family. They deserved something like that, and he knew his father would want to see their legacy after he'd been so close to leaving them all behind.

His hands shook at that thought, and he set everything down.

He hadn't been around when his dad found out he was in remission. Alex hadn't been around for a lot of things.

With a groan, he pushed back from his desk and went to his bedroom to pull on his workout gear. He needed to punch something, and he knew exactly how he was going to do that.

The sign near the front of the gym beckoned him, and he stared at it. He'd done some fights before and had come out on either side of the coin toss when it came to the bout, but this one might be a little out of his league.

Perfect.

"You're not serious," Brody said as he sidled up to Alex's side. "It might be in your weight class, but that guy has like ten years more experience than you."

Alex shrugged, something inside telling him he needed this or he'd fall down a rabbit hole that he wouldn't find his way out of.

"Don't be an idiot," Harper put in.

He hadn't been aware the other man had shown up after his shift, and that was sloppy of him. It seemed Alex was starting to get stuck in his own mind again, and that wouldn't be good for anyone.

"It's a sanctioned fight at the gym. I'm not doing an underground bout or fight club or anything."

"Well, you know the first—"

Alex glared at the other man, not letting Brody finish the line from the movie. "Not all of us are Brad Pitt."

"I still don't understand that movie," Harper put in. "Was Brad Pitt real or not?"

Alex pinched the bridge of his nose. "That movie is like what, fifteen, twenty years old? Why are we talking about it?"

"Because you're about to sign up to fight a guy with more experience than you tonight."

Alex sighed and tugged the sheet from the bulletin board. "I need to do this."

Brody searched his face. "Fuck."

Yeah, fuck. But Alex needed this. Needed *something* he could control. He didn't have much else he could at that moment, and if he could pound his body into knowing what was right or wrong, he would.

****

Tabby was just about to set out her planner on her desk at home when her phone rang. She did her best not to feel disappointed when the screen read an unknown number and not Alexander's.

She hadn't spoken to him since last night, and he hadn't shown up at the office. Her stomach ached just thinking about the fact that he might think last night was a mistake, but she'd had to work throughout the day as if nothing had happened. His brothers always saw too much, and she'd be damned if she let them know what was going on with her.

"Hello?" she said as she answered.

"Tabby? This is Brody, Alex's friend from the gym."

She frowned, worry etching it's way through her. "I remember. What can I do for you, Brody?"

The man sighed on the other end of the phone. "I got your number from Harper, who had to head out to meet his neighbor for something. I'm sorry for calling you, but I figured you'd want to know that your man is about to do something really fucking stupid."

Her man.

She didn't have a man, not really, but there was only one person who Brody would think was hers.

"Is Alexander okay?"

"For now."

She stood up quickly and grabbed her purse, sliding on her shoes at the same moment. "What's going on, Brody? Stop being so cryptic." Was

83

Alexander drinking again? No, that couldn't be it. He'd been so *strong* this past year. The only thing that had changed was...

Damn it.

No.

He was *not* going to fail at what he strived for most.

Not because of her.

"He's not drinking again if that's what you're worried about. Shit. I'm sorry. Okay, he's about to fight a guy in a bout and he's probably going to lose and end up bruised and hurt, but I think that's what our man is going for tonight. I don't know what happened between the two of you, but the guy looks like he has woman problems right now. And besides his ex, you're the only woman I know of in his life that could make him look this way. Fuck. Sorry. I'm not saying this is your fault because it's not. He's an adult, and if he's going to make a choice to fight a guy with more experience, then it's his own fault, but hell. I think he needs you, Tabby."

She gripped the phone harder and did her best not to yell at the man. He was only trying to help, after all. "What do you need me to do?"

"I'm actually on my way to your place to pick you up. I didn't know if I'd have to ask you in person to help him out or not. But that means I left him alone in the damn gym to fight that guy so I kind of want to hurry. If Harper didn't have the emergency, I know he'd have been there, too."

"How do you know where I live?"

"Harper. He had your address on file. He knows he might get fired for giving it to me, but he figured Alex was more important."

Tabby pinched the bridge of her nose. They were just trying to help, and frankly, she wasn't sure she should be driving now anyway. "How long until you get here."

A car pulled up in her driveway. "I'm here."

"I can see that." Thankful she hadn't changed into her pajamas when she'd gotten home, she ran out the front door, almost forgetting to lock it behind her. She'd come home from a long day at faking being okay and had slipped into jeans and a double tank top and hoodie because she'd wanted to be somewhat comfortable. The cold shocked her as soon as she got outside, but she kept going. She probably should have grabbed a coat, but she clearly wasn't thinking straight at the moment.

Brody had leaned over to open the passenger side door as soon as she'd run out of her house. "You should be wearing a coat."

"I wasn't thinking."

He shook his head and leaned back, reaching behind her seat to pull out a jacket. "I had a spare in here since I forgot it. It'll be big as hell on you, but at least Alex won't kick my ass for letting you get frostbite."

She tugged it over her lap and frowned. "Why do you think there's anything going on between us?"

He gave her a knowing look. "I've seen the two of you together."

She bit into her lip and watched the road as Brody drove them toward the gym. "So what exactly is he doing tonight?"

"The gym has sanctioned bouts for those who train there. They're not for prizes, or part of anything official for points or anything, but they still have people on hand in case someone gets hurt. It's not a crazy underground thing or anything."

Tabby closed her eyes. "You're not really helping right now you know."

Brody snorted. "Well, he's not really doing something smart right now either. He's been in a few fights before, but they were always with people at his level. This new guy, though? He's tougher and meaner. And he's been doing this far longer than any of us have. Because they're in the same weight class, Alex was welcome to fight him tonight if the other guy agreed, and since the other guy is a bit of an asshole, he agreed. So, yeah, the fight started about five minutes ago, and we're almost there."

She gripped Brody's jacket hard on her lap. "Will it be over by the time we get there?" she asked as she turned to look at him.

Brody let his gaze off the road for a moment when he met her eyes. "I don't know, Tabby. And honestly, I don't know *what* answer I want either."

And with that, they sat in silence as Brody sped down the street on their way to the gym.

She was so fucking angry with Alexander right now. He'd not only left her after they'd made love in her living room, he'd also neglected to contact her at all. And now he was being an idiot and using his fists instead of his words. He might not have gone back to the bottle, but he was sure finding other ways to hurt himself.

Did she want to be part of this? Did she really want to be by his side when he tried to find his footing? She'd already done that once before in her life, and it hadn't worked out. She wasn't sure if she was strong enough to do it again.

Only this was *Alexander*, damn it.

She'd loved him when she shouldn't have, and now she was falling for him all over again. This time for a man she knew and not just the man in her head she thought she knew.

She wouldn't back down, wouldn't walk away.

She just had to pray they were both strong enough to handle the consequences.

She and Brody pulled into the gym parking lot soon after she'd made that revelation and they got out of the car, practically running through the icy parking lot as she pulled on the borrowed coat. The sounds coming from the gym slammed into her as soon as they made their way in, and she didn't know what she would do once she saw him.

But she had to see him.

Brody put his hand on her elbow and led her to a spot where she could see. There was a larger crowd than she'd expected filling the gym and surrounding the ring, but there was a tiny open area near one of the corners.

Alexander's corner.

The sight of him took her breath away.

He wore black boxing gloves and dark shorts and shoes. Sweat covered his body, as did a few scrapes and blood. She wasn't sure where it was coming from, but it hurt her to see it.

Damn it. Why was he doing this to himself?

His muscles flexed as he rolled his shoulders, his body hard, unyielding, and incredibly sexy. If she weren't so freaking mad at him for daring to do this to himself, she'd want to crawl up his body like a tree and touch every single inch of him.

Suddenly, Brody's coat was too much, and she was overheated.

The other man in the ring, who looked to be about Alexander's size, rushed forward, and Tabby's eyes widened. Alexander moved so *fast,* and yet the other man moved faster. They punched at each other, a jab here, an uppercut there. She didn't know all the terms, but she knew they were going all out.

And Alexander was losing.

The sound of the gloves meeting flesh slammed into her as they hit each other over and over again. She was going to be sick, but she kept standing, knowing Alexander might need her after this.

And frankly, she wasn't going to let him walk away this time.

Damn it.

"Shit," Brody whispered under his breath.

Tabby didn't bother to look at him, her attention on the men in the ring. But she knew what Brody was cursing about. The other fighter in the ring hit Alexander square in the jaw, and the man she loved hit the ground.

He didn't get back up.

The fight was called, and cheers rang out. She only had eyes for one man. As she made her way to the edge of the ring to look at him, Alexander sat up and spat out his mouth guard. He frowned when he met her gaze, anger in his eyes, but she didn't give a shit. He could be angry all he wanted that she was there, but he didn't get to keep doing this to his body. Maybe if he'd been fighting a fair fight, she would have felt differently, but this one wasn't that, and he'd been stupid.

And she couldn't wait to tell him that.

He wasn't drinking, but he wasn't being smart either. He was fighting to feel, fighting to do *something*. And from the lean lines of his body, she knew he wasn't eating as much as he used to. Only enough to survive; not to indulge. He was healthy, but he wasn't doing anything that could become a new addiction.

She just prayed he wouldn't walk away from her.

"What are you doing here?" he growled. "And why are you wearing Brody's coat?"

She held up a hand. "Really? That's what you're going to pick a fight about now? I thought you'd have gotten the fight out of your system."

He grunted. "Not here. Not now."

"Fine. Take me to your place so I can fix you up. And don't argue."

"What about your car?" he growled, hot on her heels.

"Brody drove me because he thought you were being an idiot."

"Not here, babe."

"Don't fucking 'babe' me. Get your bag, Alexander."

He growled at her and stalked off to get his duffle from the locker room. Out of the corner of her eye, she saw Brody give her a thumbs up. As soon as Alexander stalked out of the locker room toward her, she turned on her heel and made her way to his car. The ride to his place was silent, but at least he didn't argue with her.

As soon as they got to his place, she ordered him on the chair in the kitchen, and went about cleaning him up. She didn't even bother to notice his apartment; too set on making sure he was okay. Maybe once she could breathe again, she could think about where they were and what might happen next.

What *could* happen next.

"You look terrible."

"I don't feel that great to be honest."

She gave him a worried look. "Did you hit your head hard? Do you have a concussion?"

He shook his head. "No, the doc looked me over before I left the locker room since that's protocol. That's what took me so long. No concussion, no real damage other than a few bruises."

89

He was going to have a black eye, a swollen lip, and multiple contusions all over his body. There was nothing *few* about it.

She put an ice pack on his ribs, and he sucked in a breath. "Why?"

Just one word, but there was so much in it.

She wasn't sure he was going to answer her until he opened his mouth. "Because I need to. I like to fight. I feel like I'm in control when I do. I haven't been in control of a lot of things in my life, Tabitha. But this? This I can make mine."

She let out a breath, her gaze meeting his. "Do you know the line, then? Do you?"

He swallowed hard but kept meeting her eyes. "I'm staring at it ever day."

And with that, she knew he was far stronger than he thought he was. He might be doing things she didn't understand, but he wasn't going to lose control. In fact, everything he did was because he was keeping that control locked down hard.

The only thing he couldn't control was her.

And she wasn't sure what she thought about that.

So instead of thinking—or talking—she went down to her knees.

"What are you doing?" he asked, his voice low, gruff.

"Making you feel better," she whispered as she took him out of his sweats. He was hard, long, and thick in her hand. The tips of her fingers didn't even meet at the base, and she shivered, remembering the feel of him inside. "I didn't get to do this before. And because I had to watch you fight, I get to do this now. I get to be the one in control."

He licked his lips, wincing as he went over the cut, and slid his hand through her hair, the ice long forgotten on the table. "I'm clean. I had the doctors check me, but I've only been with one woman, Tabitha. And well...I'm clean. For this, I'm clean."

She let out a breath; grateful he was so careful with her.

"I'm not going to be able to reciprocate tonight, not with my lip like this."

She squeezed him, loving the way his eyes crossed.

"I don't need you to. Not tonight." She took a deep breath. "Next time, though. Okay?"

He tugged on her hair softly. "Next time," he whispered.

She licked the tip of his dick in response, and he groaned. He was hurting, so she didn't make it last long, didn't tease him until they were both panting with need this time. They could do that later. For now, she just wanted to pleasure him because it pleased her at the same time. He was too big for her to swallow, so she used her hands to take the rest of him.

Slow and easy.

Then fast and hard.

And when he came in her mouth, he tried to pull away, but she didn't let him.

She wanted all of him.

When she was finished, he stood up, tucked himself back in his sweats, and lifted her into his arms.

"Your ribs!"

"They aren't broken, not even bruised. Just a little sore. I'm taking you to bed so we can sleep. And in the middle of the night, I'm going to make love to you because that's what we both need, what we both want."

"Okay," she breathed.

She curled into him as he carried her, feeling cherished beyond measure but knowing everything could change in an instant. They hadn't spoken about what they were doing and what could come next. But they would.

And she'd fight for him, just like she would fight for herself.

Because sometimes it took looking at another person in another stage of their life to understand exactly what you wanted. And this time, it was Tabby's turn to figure that out.

STORM

Storm slammed the door closed behind him and tried to contain his anger. It wasn't easy when he wanted to fucking punch something. How in the hell had his family become this? They used to be okay, used to be able to walk down a road without shit coming at them from all sides. Yet over the past few years, almost every single person in his family had gone through something.

Some had made it out the other side, bloody and bruised, but alive.

And yet with his baby brother, he didn't know if there was an end in sight. Alex might be out of rehab, but Storm had seen the bruises on the other man's face tonight. He'd seen the wary look in his eyes when Storm and Wes had confronted him. Alex might not be drinking, but fighting like he was couldn't be healthy.

Not to mention Storm knew damn well there was something going on between Alex and Tabby. He saw the looks, saw the heat. Others might have missed it, but Storm had spent the past two years keeping his eye on Alex. Storm had fucked up before by not acting sooner when Alex had fallen, but he'd be damned if he failed as a brother again.

Austin might be the oldest of the Montgomerys, but Storm took his responsibility as next in line seriously. Wes might only be a few minutes older, but Storm didn't count those. His younger siblings had gone through hell before settling down, and now it was Storm's job to make sure Alex found his peace.

Because if he didn't...

Storm didn't want to think about the outcome.

The doorbell rang, and Storm frowned before going to answering it. Jillian stood on the other side, a six-pack in her hand and a glare on her face.

"Today was a shit-tastic day, and since I'm a plumber, I literally mean shit." She pushed past him and he shook his head.

He and Jillian had been dating off and on for a while now, but it was nothing too serious. They were friends who, when they had time and inclination, slept together. They were fucking amazing together, it was true, but they'd both had the talk long ago that they were better off as friends who gave great orgasms than something serious.

Part of that was why he hadn't offered her a job at Montgomery Inc. though they needed a plumber. In fact, even if he offered it, he knew she'd say no. Their goal was to be uncomplicated and sleep together whenever they felt like it, and working together would be fucking idiotic.

"Drink this," Jillian said as she thrust a beer into his hand. "I just showered and I'm cranky. But I don't know why *you're* cranky."

"Alex is fighting," he said softly.

Jillian's eyes rounded. "Well, fuck. Tell me everything."

And that's why he was friends with her. He *could* tell her everything. He knew it would be easier if they loved each other, if they both saw a future. But they didn't, and frankly, they wouldn't.

But when his head was a mess like this, worrying about a thousand other things, he would take Jillian as she was because he knew she would do the same.

It was all he had, and hell, that was way better than nothing.

CHAPTER SEVEN

It had been a couple of weeks since he'd first had Tabitha in his arms, in his bed, and yet Alex still couldn't get her out of his mind. It didn't help that they'd spent every night together, even if they didn't sleep over each time. They were still feeling each other out, still figuring out what it all meant.

But he knew he could drown in her if he weren't careful.

And even though he thought he could survive that, he didn't want to bring Tabitha down with him—not if it meant hurting her in the process.

In the two weeks since the fight, his bruises had healed, and he'd kept the worst of them from his family, but the twins had seen them. He didn't want to keep secrets from the Montgomerys anymore, but neither did he want to show up to a family dinner with a black eye. He wasn't sure he could handle the questions.

Wes and Storm hadn't been angry, but now they knew where he worked out and what he was training for. He figured they'd be at the next bout, and there was no stopping that. By now, the entire family probably knew, but they were giving him space. He wasn't sure what he felt about that since they usually didn't give anyone space. Either they were being careful with him, or they didn't know what to do with him.

Honestly, he figured it was a bit of both.

Now he was sitting in his sister's house with most of the men of his immediate family surrounding him for a guys' night. The women had had their night the week before, so this time, it was all about the Montgomery men and those that had married into the family while the others watched the children of the large crew.

"What are you doing over there?" Wes asked, a frown on his face. "You're being all introspective, and it's guys' night. No thinking at guys' night."

Jake, his brother-in-law, snorted. "Oh, that's a good one. Just don't tell my wife that."

Border, Jake's husband and third in their relationship with Alex's sister Maya, laughed. "*Our* wife already figures that."

Alex shook his head, a grin on his face. "I'm sorry for thinking. I promise to only grunt and scratch myself from now on."

Decker tilted his beer toward Alex. "Good man. But don't forget to eat and talk sports. Manly stuff."

Griffin rolled his eyes and sat down next to Decker. "Considering Austin, Luc, *and* you just had a twenty-minute conversation about baby wipes, I'm pretty sure we don't fit the mold."

Alex sipped his iced tea and held back a smile. Most of the men in the room were now fathers, and it surprised him how much things had changed over the past few years. Austin had a wife and two children, Decker had married Miranda and had had baby Micah a few months ago. Luc had married Meghan and helped raise her two kids from her previous marriage with her asshole ex-husband and also had the new baby, Emma. Jake and Border had not only married each other, but Maya, as well, before having Noah around the same time Emma and Micah were born.

Hell, even Griffin had eloped with Autumn, surprising them all.

Only the twins and he were left, though Alex had already been married before and wanted nothing to do with that in the future. Of course, as soon as he thought that, Tabitha's face entered his mind, but he quickly pushed that out of the way.

He didn't know exactly what he was doing with her, but he wasn't sure marriage was a possibly. Not with his track record.

Storm sank down into the couch next to Alex and let out a sigh.

"Doing okay?" Alex asked, grateful his brother had pulled him out of his thoughts. They'd been heading into dangerous territory, and he wanted to focus on the present, not on what could happen next and what *had* happened to bring him here.

Storm shot him a look before glaring over at Wes, who flipped him off. "This fucker over here decided to start on the Richmond site a day early because of a shift later on down the line that would have caused problems. But because we weren't exactly ready for it and are stretched a bit thin with a few guys being sick thanks to the cold, Tab couldn't get most of the other guys on this site in time."

Alex ignored the way just hearing Tabitha's name was like a kick to the chest. He didn't like it, nor did he know what to do about it.

"Meaning lazy ass over there actually had to work," Wes drawled.

"Fuck you," Storm bit out, holding his shoulder.

"For the record, I lift more than both of you daily so stop whining," Decker put in. "And, Storm, if you hurt so much, why don't you ask your girlfriend to rub you down?"

Alex snorted, a smile crawling over his face.

"Yeah, why don't you tell us about Jillian?" It felt good to be joking with his family again, though he wasn't sure he was ready to have the attention focused on him and talk about Tabitha yet. It was complicated since she worked with his family, and hell, they hadn't even talked about who they were together yet. They'd done really well avoiding talking about that at all.

Probably not a good sign.

"Shut it," Storm said with an odd look in his eyes. "Jillian and I are just hanging out."

"Sleeping together is more than hanging out," Austin said.

Storm sighed. "We're keeping it casual. We're both busy as hell, and it makes it hard to see each other. We're friends who happen to have sex when we both want to. And now that I've talked about my feelings, can we get the chili out of the crockpot, or are you going to ask how the sex is?"

"Well," Jake crooned. "Since you brought it up."

Border punched him in the side, and Jake blushed at whatever the other man whispered in his ear. Alex grinned and took another drink of his tea.

Damn, he'd missed this.

They ate chili and wings and other things that were horrible for them and talked about kids, games, and whatever was going on at work. None of them were in their early twenties anymore, so they didn't eat like this often. But when they did, it was usually when they were together. As for Alex, he ate a full portion but didn't go back for seconds. The food tasted too good, and he didn't want to end up eating his way through the whole damn table.

Storm checked his phone right about the time Alex was going to head out and grinned.

"What?"

"Jillian is here to pick me up," Storm explained, his voice low. But he hadn't spoken softly enough, apparently.

"She's only your friend, huh?" Wes said with a wide smile. "I want to meet her. How come none of us have met her?"

Storm pinched the bridge of his nose. "She's busy. She's working her ass off on her current job right now, and it sucks ass, so stop pestering. Okay? My truck is in the shop because I not only needed new winter tires, but there was something off when I started it this morning. She dropped me off at work, but you were the one to drive me here, Wes, if you recall."

Wes shrugged. "I figured I'd drive you home, too. No big deal. But come on, have her come in." Wes fluttered his eyelashes, and Alex barked off a laugh, surprised he'd laughed and smiled as much as he had this evening.

The others stared at him for a moment, and he swallowed. Apparently, the others had noticed he'd laughed more tonight than usual, as well.

"I'll text her," Storm grumped, his eyes narrowed. "But don't fuck around with her, got me? She's a good woman, and my friend."

Wes put up his hands. "I'm not going to be a bastard to a woman you're dating, Storm. But if she's here, she might as well meet the horde."

Storm flipped off the room as he texted with one hand. "This is going to be interesting," he mumbled.

Alex slid his hands into his pockets and waited as Storm stalked toward the front door and opened it.

The first thing he heard was bright laughter as a slender blonde woman walked into the house. She had on work boots and jeans, plus an old coat that seemed far too big for her. He only knew she was slender from her face and legs.

"I didn't realize you were all as big as Storm," she blurted, and the guys laughed. The tension that had filled the room at Storm's text popped like a balloon.

"Well, some of us are bigger," Jake said with a grin, and Jillian rolled her eyes.

"Sure, honey, whatever you say."

Alex liked her already.

"So, yeah, these are the guys," Storm put in. "Guys, this is Jillian."

"Hi, Jillian," the guys said as one before breaking out into laughter.

Jillian grinned. "Hi, guys. Do you have names, or do you walk around like some bearded boy band? You know, the one after the third album where they aren't straight cookie cutter anymore and are trying for something a little edgier."

"I still stay Backstreet Boys were better than N'SYNC," Jake put in.

"New Kids on the Block," Austin said with a wince. "And how the hell do I know that name?"

"Aren't they touring now?" Alex asked, running a hand through his hair. "And how the hell do I know *that*?"

"Run, Jillian," Griffin said deadpan. "Run before they show you their love for O-Town."

Jillian held up her hands, laughter in her eyes. "I'm sorry I mentioned boy bands. I'm learning *way* more than I thought I would."

Storm let out a breath and put his arm around Jillian's shoulder. She hip-bumped him and laughed. "We're out of here. And just so you know, I'm cutting you all out of my life for talking about boy bands just now."

Alex nodded solemnly. "I understand. It's because you're a One Direction fan, right? You must be cut up that they broke up."

Storm flipped him off, and the guys broke out into chuckles as he pulled Jillian out the door.

"Nice to meet you!" she called, but they didn't get a chance to say anything back since Storm slammed the door shut.

There was an awkward silence after that as the guys looked at one another.

"How much will it cost for us not to tell the women about this conversation?" Austin asked.

Silence.

"That's what I thought," his eldest brother grumbled. "Fuck."

"It's not our fault," Griffin put in. "With the twenty-four-hour news cycle, we have to listen to hours of election coverage crap and celebrity gossip. Things are bound to stick."

"Right," Alex put in. "We'll just go with that."

The guys shook their heads and finished cleaning up before everyone headed out. Alex's chest felt lighter than it had in years. He'd had a whole evening where no one had been worried outwardly about drinking in front of him, and he hadn't actually wanted a drink once. He'd been too distracted by conversations with his family and thinking about Tabitha to want to sneak into the kitchen for a beer.

He counted that as progress.

He pulled up to Tabitha's place before he'd even thought about his destination. He hadn't called or texted to ask her if she was even home, but he saw the light on in the living room. She might be busy, and if that were the case, he'd leave, but he wanted to see her.

And he didn't want to think about *why* he wanted to see her so much.

She opened the door after the first knock, her eyes warm. "Was boys' night fun?"

He nodded, his hands stuffed in his pockets. "Is it okay I'm here?" he asked. "I didn't call."

She smiled and stepped back. "You're always welcome. Always."

He didn't know what to do with the emotions swelling inside him at her words.

"Did you eat? I have some leftover chicken in the fridge if you didn't," she said as she closed the front door behind them.

Alex moved toward her and cupped her cheek. She smiled at him and leaned into his hold. What had he done to deserve a woman like her looking at him like she was? Nothing, he knew. He hadn't done a damn thing. But he was sure as fuck going to be selfish and take what he could. And if he had anything left to give, she could have it.

"I ate a bunch of junk food and things horrible for me at Maya's."

She snorted and played her fingers along his abs. "Junk food is good for you every once in a while."

He laughed. "Really? What nutritionist says that?"

"I say it," she explained. "Sometimes, you need to give in to the food and laughter so you can unwind. I know you're very careful about what you put into your body, but knowing you *can* have a chip or five and not go crazy means something."

He nodded, aware she knew more about him than he realized. She'd noticed how careful he was about what he ate, and he wasn't sure how he felt about that.

"Did I make you mad?" she whispered. "For commenting on that?"

He shook his head and played with her hair. "No." He paused. He hadn't told her a lot about what he was thinking, and that was a disservice to them both. "I started watching what I eat in rehab. I used to not care what I put into my body. Cake, fried foods, soda, booze." She wrapped her arms around his waist loosely, and he relaxed a bit. "I worked out a lot so I didn't end up with a huge gut, but I was never as in shape as the rest of my family. But when I was in rehab, I watched some of the other guys turn to smoking or eating more than they used to in order to keep the cravings for something harder at bay. I didn't want to replace one kind of craving for another."

She nodded and looked like she wanted to say something more but didn't.

He was well aware that fighting like he was and being as careful about what he ate weren't exactly crutches, but they probably weren't the best for him either. He just had to take things one day at a time.

And honestly, those two things weren't the addictions he had to be careful about.

It was the woman in his arms.

Just one taste, and he knew he'd be addicted to her forever.

And that scared him more than what he ate or if another fighter could kick his ass.

But Alex had never truly been good at doing what was right for him, and hell, he wasn't sure if Tabitha was *wrong* for him.

He didn't care.

He wanted her.

And when she lifted onto her toes to kiss his chin, her eyes warm pools of desire, he knew she wanted him, as well.

He cupped the back of her head. "I didn't come here for this," he whispered. "I don't know why I came, actually."

She ran her hands up his back, her nails digging in. "That's okay. You're not taking if I'm giving it freely."

He kissed her slowly, her lips soft velvet against his own. "Let's go slow this time."

She smiled, a small movement against the seam of his lips. "You said that last time. And the time before. And we never go slow."

He ran his hand down her side and back up again to cup her breast. When he flicked his thumb over her nipple, she shivered in his hold. "We can try for slow. But you're so fucking hot in my arms that it's hard for me to *stay* slow once I have you."

She reached between them and cupped him. His eyes crossed, and he let out a rough laugh. "What if I don't want to go slow?" she purred.

He liked this Tabitha. The fiery one in his arms that no one else saw. He didn't know what that said about him and his feelings for her, but right then, he couldn't think with her tit in his hand and her hand on his dick.

He kissed her again, his tongue sliding along hers in an erotic caress. "Slow," he whispered. He kissed down her neck, pulling her collar away from her body so he could lick her shoulder. "Slow."

She ran her hands up his back again, and he ground into her. They both froze at the feel of the rigid line of his cock pressing into her belly.

"Well, hell, so much for slow," he said with a laugh.

"We can go slow," she breathed. "I promise."

He tucked her hair back from her face again. "Yeah?" He let out a breath. "I haven't even taken you out on a date, Tabitha. What is wrong with me? And our training sessions at the gym don't count."

She frowned. "They count in terms of being helpful, at least. And I don't care about dates right now. I just want you in my bed tonight. We can...we can go on a date tomorrow. Or the next night. Just take me tonight, okay?"

He licked his lips. "So we're dating, then?"

She let out a low laugh. "Yeah, I guess we are. Is it weird we didn't talk about that before now?"

He shook his head. "Only if we make it weird. And I think we were doing a good job of *not* talking about it at all before this."

She pulled his head down and kissed him hard on the mouth. "So, boyfriend?"

His heart sped up at the word. He'd only been a boyfriend to one other person, and she'd broken him beyond repair. But he could do this. He could.

"And I think I just scared you. No labels?"

He shook his head, noticing the sadness in her eyes that she couldn't quite hide. "Labels work. I just..." He let out a breath. Time to be honest, right? "I've only had one other girlfriend." The last part was whispered so low he was afraid she wouldn't hear him. Maybe that would be for the best.

Her eyes widened fractionally, but she gave him a nod. "I didn't think about that. You were young when—" She cut herself off. "Okay, boyfriend, we can go on a date, and you can buy me a milkshake or something later. But for now, I *really* want to see if we can go slow." She cupped him again, and he groaned. "What do you say?"

She always knew the right thing to say, and he would be grateful for that even if it confused him.

In answer to her question, he lifted her into his arms and carried her to the bedroom, his mouth on hers the entire time. He needed her more than he cared to admit, and while that scared him—and it should—he knew that he wouldn't be able to let her go...even if it was the best thing for both of them.

He set her down on her feet at the foot of the bed and slowly stripped her out of her clothes, kissing her skin as soon as he bared each part of her. He licked down her shoulders, nibbling at her inner arm until she squirmed. Then he moved to the tops of her breasts that lay above the cups of her bra. He licked them, sucked, and bit down gently before going to his knees so he could do the same to her stomach.

Her skin was so soft, so perfect. "I want to lick every inch of you," he growled into her hip.

She ran her hand through his hair and smiled down at him. "You're on your way to doing so. Will you take off your shirt? I want to touch your skin."

Because she asked, he did, keeping his eyes on hers the whole time. She licked her lips, and he smiled before pressing kisses to her hipbones above the top of her jeans. She had wide hips that were perfect for his hands, and he loved the fact that every time he fucked her from behind, he got to grip on to her ass and push in deeper. Her butt would move with him, jiggling just right. His ex had been stick thin, and while he loved women's bodies in general, he found himself wanting Tabitha's more.

"Lay down on the bed," he growled, annoyed with himself for thinking of Jessica just then. "I want to feast on you."

She blushed but did as he asked. She still wore her bra, jeans, and panties, but he'd take care of them soon. For now, he wanted her breasts since he rarely got to spend much time with them. They were always moving too fast for him to truly give them their due attention.

He crawled over her, and she smiled up at him lazily. When he lifted her up slightly to unclasp her bra, she gripped his shoulders and licked her lips. Since they looked so enticing, he captured them with his own, deepening the kiss as he took off her bra completely.

When she was bare before him, he lowered her fully to the bed and began kissing her nipples just as he had her mouth. She arched into him when he plumped her breasts in his hands, holding them together and molding them before biting and sucking on each nipple in turn. She moaned, her body going sweat-slick as he bit down harder, sucking, licking, and nibbling until he was sure she was almost ready to come.

"I...I can't come just from my breasts," she gasped. "I need something. Touch me, please."

He kissed up her neck and then took her mouth again. "Is that a challenge?"

She narrowed her eyes at him. "I'll touch myself if I have to, Alexander Montgomery. Now get me off."

He laughed and went down to her breasts once more, aware her hand was creeping down to the apex of her thighs. Well, he couldn't have that. He gripped her wrist in his hand and brought it up to and over her head. Even as she grumbled, she arched again, his attention never leaving her breasts. She was so close, but he knew that she might need a little more urging. So he shifted to lean on his elbow even as he used that arm to hold her down and took his free hand and slid it over her jeans where the heat of her nearly scalded him.

Just one touch, and she broke apart in his arms.

She was so fucking beautiful when she came.

A goddess in his arms.

In his life.

While she came down from her high, he quickly stripped her out of her pants and underwear and spread her legs. She was still coming as he pressed his mouth to her and licked.

She screamed, her hips pressing into him, and he sucked and licked at her cunt. She tasted so fucking sweet, he knew he could get lost between the silk of her inner thighs forever. He speared her with two fingers, even as he licked at her clit, her juices coating his face and his beard. He wanted her to come again, wanted her to buck against his face as she lost control.

"Come on, baby. Come on my face. Show me how fucking hot you are when I have my mouth on your pretty little cunt. Play with your nipples for me, and I'll reward you with my cock."

She looked down at him, her eyes dark, and a seductive smile on her face as she slowly cupped her breasts.

"That's it. Pluck at them. Imagine it's my fingers."

"Less talking," she panted. "More eating."

He chuckled then and went back to his feast, licking up her lips and darting his tongue in and out of her along with three of his fingers. She was so tight that he knew he was stretching her, but he had to make sure she would be ready for him when he slid himself inside.

She came again when he bit down gently on her clit, and he lapped at her before pulling back and flipping her over on her stomach. She let out a shriek, and he slapped her ass.

"Hey!" she said as she looked over her shoulder. "Did you just spank me?"

He winked and shucked off his pants, bending down to pick up the condom he'd put in his pocket earlier. "Yeah. Want me to do it again?"

She blushed and gave him a thoughtful look. "Maybe."

He grinned and smacked her ass one more time before pulling on her thighs so she was on all fours. "I like the way you think." He lowered his head and licked at her cunt, using his hands to spread her before him. She lowered her head on the bed, pressing her ass closer to his face. He licked up and played with her hole, enjoying the way she squirmed. He used her wetness to prepare her as he slowly entered the tip of his finger inside. She gasped, her body stiffening, and he bit one cheek.

"Relax, baby, I'm not going to fuck your ass tonight."

"But you will later?" she asked.

"If you want." He wanted, that was for sure.

"I don't know. I just know I like whatever you're doing to me, even if it's new."

He kissed her lower back as he worked her slowly before removing his finger. "You can have me whenever you're ready. And if you're not ever ready, that's okay, too. It's all about what you want?"

She looked over her shoulder as he positioned himself at her entrance. "And what about what you want?"

He blinked at the intensity of her words. "I want you." Honest. Open. And the only thing he could think of at the moment...and maybe ever.

"I want you, too." A whispered plea.

He covered her back with his body and kissed her mouth. "You can have me." He swallowed hard as he filled her, aware that this wasn't just fucking, wasn't just sex on a cold night. But it never had been with Tabitha, and he figured it never would be.

That should scare him more than it did, but right then, all he could think of was the sweetness of her in his arms, over him, under him, around him, and the feel of her pussy clenching his cock. He gripped her ass, holding her firmly to him, and he slowly thrust in and out of her. He'd promised slow, and damn it, he would give her slow.

Alex rolled his hips, loving the way she looked over her shoulder at him. But he wanted more, he wanted to *see* her, so he pulled out fully and gently shifted her so she was on her back and in the middle of the bed. He covered her with his body and took her hand in his, guiding it to the base of his cock.

"Slide me in, baby. Take me."

She licked her lips, her eyes wet and dark, and did as he asked, slowly guiding him into her. His breaths came in pants, sweat rolling down his back as he achingly entered her inch by inch. And when he was fully seated, they both lay there, connected in more ways than he ever thought possible. He tangled his fingers with hers and began to move.

They made love, their hands clasped, their eyes on each other, as he put his weight on his elbows so as not to touch her.

And when they came together, Alex knew he was in trouble.

She wasn't his addiction, wasn't his pain.

She was everything else and everything he never thought possible.

And that was scarier than the idea of wanting the bottle.

CHAPTER EIGHT

Tabby's head hurt, and her thighs were sore, but damn if she didn't feel on top of the world. Not only did she and Alexander have a date planned for the next day but she'd also finished everything on her to-do list for the day with an hour to spare. And since she loved her lists, that meant she'd done about a hundred different things today and still wasn't tired. There was truly nothing better than checking something off or highlighting something on a list once it was completed. It was its own kind of euphoria.

Of course, that made her think of a certain man in her bed and how many times she'd come from his mouth alone.

So maybe there *were* a few things better than a to-do list.

Most of the guys had left for their other sites but since the incident involving the former client, no one had let her stay in the office alone. Their overprotectiveness might annoy her, but she was so used to it with her three brothers, she'd learned to live with it. And if any of them ever went too far and stifled her, she'd fight back. For now, she'd let them worry and act like mother hens because it made them feel better. And if she were honest with herself, it made her feel better, too. There might be even greater security on the place, and she was training to protect herself, but it still wasn't enough.

Not yet.

"I need to head out," Storm said as he walked to her desk. "Alex is in the back printing something so you aren't alone, but do you want me to stay a bit longer?"

She shook her head and tried not to look at Alexander as he strode into the room, a stack of papers in his hand. They hadn't told the others they were seeing each other, and it had been a mutual decision. It would get messy and complicated quickly once the Montgomerys knew. And heck, it was already pretty messy.

From the look in Storm's eyes, however, she had a feeling he might be on to them. This particular Montgomery always saw too much. Damn the man.

"She's fine with me," Alexander put in, his voice low. "Go head on out. We'll lock up."

Storm raised a brow at Alexander speaking for her, and she shrugged. "Well, he's right. I'm almost done anyway. So go work, and let me be." He narrowed his eyes, and she sighed. "But thank you for being all big brother on me and making sure I'm safe. I appreciate it. However, please keep in mind that I have three older siblings in Pennsylvania, and I'm not sure I have room for more."

Storm folded his arms over his broad chest. "They're not here, are they? And the Montgomerys took you in so you have to deal with all of us acting like big brothers."

She couldn't help but meet Alexander's eyes at that, and he raised a brow.

All of us? Those eyes seemed to ask.

Definitely not all of them.

"She's good, Storm," Alexander grumbled, and she couldn't help but smile at him. He was such a grumpy bear when his brothers put on the tough-guy act.

Storm gave her a look, and she held back a sigh. Yeah, there was no hiding her feelings anymore from this particular Montgomery, and all three of them knew it. But when Storm left without another word, she figured he would keep their secret.

"He won't tell the others if we don't want him to," Alexander said when he stepped toward her. They didn't touch since there were cameras first-off, and they'd both decided to try and keep work separate from their relationship.

She bit her lip. "Do we want them to know? I mean, I kind of like that this is just between you and me for now. Don't get me wrong, I *love* your family, but things tend to become big once everyone knows."

He nodded and leaned against her desk. "And I already have them looking at me with caution these days. I'd rather find a balance with you without their worry."

She sucked in a breath, aware he was sharing with her more than he had before. The fact that he was an alcoholic hadn't been a secret between them since she'd known him throughout it all, but he was starting to open up more and more about it.

Maybe it was time for her to share more about herself, as well.

"Are you doing anything tonight?" she asked, changing the subject when his face went a little sad.

He shook his head. "No, what do you have in mind?"

She let out a breath and met his gaze. "I'd like to go back out to the streets where I saw you. I want to tell you why I was there." It was time. She knew so many of his secrets because they'd been strewn about him when he'd hit rock bottom, but he didn't know many of hers. It was only fair, and she felt like it was time to show him a little more of herself. It wouldn't be easy, and she was actually a little scared, but she prayed everything would be okay in the end.

He stood up straight and studied her face. "Dinner first? Then I'd be honored for you to share with me what you need to."

She licked her lips and started to pack up, knowing that this was a big step in a direction she hoped both of them were prepared for. "Dinner first," she repeated once she'd grabbed everything.

She could do this.

She had to.

After dinner, they pulled into one of the parking lots downtown and paid. It was cold but not as frigid as it had been. That had to count for something.

"So," he began as he took her hand. "Want to tell me what you do out here?"

She nodded, holding the large bag she'd kept in her car close to her. "Every week I go to shelters and feed the homeless. When I have time and when it's warmer, I walk the streets, feeding who I can...and looking."

He squeezed her hand. "Looking for who?"

"Looking for my ex and his child."

He froze, and she almost tripped, but his hand kept her steady. "What?"

She turned to him and met his gaze. "About five years ago, I met a man named Michael. We fell in love, and I also fell in love with his daughter, Angel. His wife had died from cancer a couple of years before, and Michael and Angel had done okay for those two years on their own. When Angel was five, I came across her while I was finishing my degree and working for the Montgomerys part-time. She was so cute and funny. She was at the park where I was reading, and I fell in love with her right then. Michael was there, watching her, and he came over to talk. Soon we began dating, and somehow, he and Angel ended up moving in with me."

Alexander's eyes widened. "I knew you then," he whispered. "And yet I didn't know any of this."

She shook her head. "None of you did. My family knew because I was close to them, but I didn't end up close to the Montgomerys until...until later." She let out a breath and pulled at his hand. They kept walking, and while she told the story, she also paid attention to their surroundings, doing her best to look for those she had lost. "The first couple of months were an adjustment, but wonderful in retrospect. It wasn't until month three that I realized Michael was a functioning alcoholic."

She said the words quickly, but Alexander still cursed at her side. Yes, she saw the parallels here, but damn it, Michael and Alexander were two different people, and they had both gone about things differently. He would just have to see that.

"Stop it," she said softly. "He isn't you. You got help. He...he didn't."

Alexander stopped them under an awning and forced her to look at him. "Tell me the rest," he bit out.

"He never stopped drinking and was never completely sober. I didn't catch the signs because, apparently, I had never seen him without something in his system and he was *really* good at hiding it."

"We get like that."

"Stop comparing yourself to him."

"I can't help it, Tabitha."

She cupped his face with her gloved hand, but he didn't pull away. That had to count for something. "He turned into a horrible person I couldn't live with, and I found out later, someone I never truly loved. How could I love a man I didn't actually know? Though it killed me, I had to ask him to leave when the only time he spoke to me was to yell at me. He took Angel with him. I talked to lawyers and everything, trying to think about what to do with Angel, but I had no rights. And though a social worker came to see what they could do because my brother had connections in the city, it was too late. Michael and Angel were gone. I had no idea where they had moved to until I got a letter from Angel."

She sucked in a breath, and Alexander cupped her face in turn. "Go on."

"She remembered my address," Tabby whispered. "*Her* old address. She somehow found a stamp and an envelope and mailed it to me. But there wasn't a return address because she doesn't *have* an address. Apparently, she and Michael have been living on the streets for four years, sometimes finding small apartments to live in if they could. I'm not sure what they do or how they do it, but I still get letters sometimes." Letters she held close. "The courts can't do anything for Angel because they can't find her. But I'm not going to stop looking." She swallowed hard. "Angel doesn't deserve this." Tears slid down her cheeks. "I shouldn't have kicked Michael out, but I didn't know what else to do. And because I did, Angel's out in the cold."

Alexander tucked her close, and she cried in his arms. "I'll help you look, baby. No kid deserves that."

She held on to him and tried to stop the tears, but she couldn't. She'd never told anyone the whole story. Not even her family knew she searched as hard as she did.

He pushed her back slightly to look her in the face, and she pressed her lips together. She couldn't read him, couldn't figure out if this would be too much. Alexander might be an alcoholic, but he'd found the strength to ask for help and to stay the course with that help.

Michael hadn't been able to and was hurting Angel in the process. She saw the difference, but she didn't know if Alexander did.

There was something else in his eyes, an old hurt she couldn't name, but she knew this wasn't the right time to ask about it.

The two of them had so much going against them, so many obstacles that seemed almost insurmountable. She only prayed they had enough between them elsewhere to make it. Because though she'd been with Michael before, it had been the quiet Montgomery she'd fallen for first when she'd been too young to know what to do about it. He'd been married, and she'd stayed away because it would be foolish to do anything else.

Only now, things were different. She was the one in his arms. He was the one holding her. But what if she had too much baggage? What if she wasn't enough?

She hadn't been before.

And damn it, she didn't want to end up the same way...again.

****

Alex ran a hand through his hair and tried to wake up fully. Tabitha had left less than an hour ago to change clothes. Neither one of them had slept much the night before. They hadn't had sex, but had held each other all night as they talked about possible options.

It had surprised the hell out of him that Tabitha had lived with another man before.

Just like it had surprised the hell out of him that Michael had been an alcoholic.

It wasn't the same, she'd said.

It isn't the same, he told himself.

And yet, he knew that no matter how they danced around the issue, there were too many similarities, and he couldn't quite go back to the way things were before. Of course, no matter what she shared with him, they wouldn't have been able to go back.

They'd become closer over time, so fucking close. And he didn't know what to do with that. He honestly hurt for her, and it killed him that she'd been in that situation.

Alex rolled his neck on his shoulders, trying to get the kinks out. But no matter what he did, he couldn't remove the stress that came from the conversation and revelations he'd had with Tabitha the night before. They'd both been emotionally wrung out, but he hadn't even told her exactly *why*. He knew that if they were to continue down the path they seemed to be on, he'd have to tell her everything, but he wasn't sure he could. He'd never told a soul about his demons, not even his sponsor or his therapist. Both of them knew that whatever Alex hid was bad—beyond bad—but they worked with him outside of those secrets.

It wasn't lost on him that if he perhaps told someone about what had happened, it might help, but he wasn't sure he could form the words. He didn't want to think about it, didn't want to let those memories come back and become any sharper than they already were.

But he had a feeling if he were going to open up to anyone it would be *her*.

She'd told him about Michael and Angel, and he'd held her when she cried. She'd told him her secrets, her fears, and yet he hadn't shared everything with her. It wasn't lost on him that he'd told her more than he'd told anyone else outside those in his meetings and at rehab, but with Tabitha, it was different.

It would always be different with her.

Letting out a sigh, he moved to the kitchen to make some coffee. He desperately needed caffeine, and he figured he'd make enough for when Tabitha came back. It was the weekend, and while both of them usually worked on odd projects, today they had decided to take the morning off to just relax.

Maybe *relax* wasn't the best word since neither of them could really relax after the night prior, but he figured if she needed time to walk around the park or sit in front of the TV with him, he could do that much.

Before he started drinking as much, he'd never really been someone who shared what they were feeling. Yeah, he'd been a little better before everything went to hell than he was now, but not by much. He was at least trying to be more open these days, but he hadn't yet jumped that hurdle, and he wasn't sure he'd ever be ready to.

He'd started drinking to silence the pain, the demons, and hadn't stopped until he'd not only hurt himself but also the people he loved. If it hadn't been for the looks on his family's faces when he hit rock bottom, he might have never stopped. He'd have drunk himself to death, and he would have been too damn numb to notice. But a small part of him had actually cared about what his family saw, what the *children* saw, and he'd finally let Maya and Jake take him to rehab.

Alex sipped his coffee, trying to get the bitter taste of regret off his tongue.

He would always be grateful to be a Montgomery, even if he hadn't lived up to the name. They'd saved his life, and now, he figured he should start living it. Only he wasn't sure he would ever be good enough for Tabitha. Damn it, he *knew* he wouldn't be good enough. She'd fought for herself in her last relationship, and fought every damn week for the child she hadn't been able to save. He had to admire that strength, even as he was a little envious of it.

The doorbell rang, and Alex frowned at the clock. Tabitha had been quick if she was already back, but maybe she was just going comfy today with what she wore. He didn't mind since that meant he could probably get away with wearing sweats all day as they vegged out. A small smile claimed his lips, and he let it stay there. After all the shit she'd been through recently, she deserved a day to be lazy and watch movies. And he was kind of glad she wanted to spend the day with him.

He set his coffee down on the counter and went to answer the door, an odd spring in his step. Hell, even after everything that came out last night and the path his thoughts had gone down today so far, just thinking of Tabitha made him...*happy*. That should have worried him, but right then, he only wanted to keep that smile and make her smile in return.

When he opened the door, however, all thoughts of happiness fled from his mind and his smile slid off his face, a scowl taking its place.

"What the fuck do you think you're doing here?" Rage filled his veins even as a wave of pain slammed into him with the force of a two-ton truck. Sweat started to run down his back, and his stomach twisted, bile churning as it rose in his throat.

His ex-wife, Jessica, stood on the other side of his front door, her hair put together just so, her makeup looking perfect as always. She wore a pair of tan leggings tucked into furry boots and a matching furry jacket. She had on earmuffs that even had the same tawny fur on them, and he knew she never wore hats because she hated messing up her hair. With how long she'd taken every morning to do it, he hadn't blamed her, even when he'd thought it was her own fault when she inevitably caught a cold from not wearing enough layers.

And when Jessica caught a cold, the entire world felt her wrath. People might joke about the Man Cold, but it had nothing on Jessica. Even when he'd been working two jobs to keep a roof over their heads when they'd first been married, he'd still had to take care of her and wait on her hand and foot when she had the slightest sniffle. But he'd been so damn in love and lust with her, that he hadn't cared about the lack of sleep. And taking care of your wife when she's sick in bed is just a natural thing to do. At the time, it hadn't mattered that her being down with a slight cough that turned out to be nothing meant he had to miss work. He'd loved her, and wanted to make sure she was treated like the princess she thought she was.

He hadn't minded all of that then, but now, he just wanted to kick himself for falling into her traps.

Fuck.

She wasn't always evil, he reminded himself. He hadn't always been a fucking idiot when it came to her.

Or maybe all of that was a lie.

"Aren't you going to invite me in?" she asked, her voice grating on him. She used that high tone she'd picked up over the last few years. When they'd been in high school, she'd been a little softer with her voice, and a little softer everywhere else. During their marriage, however, she'd started working out daily and watching everything she ate. While he might do that now, it wasn't to her extremes.

There was nothing soft about her anymore.

And he had to think that some of that was his fault.

He hated that it had come to this. Though he and his sister both had exes that were truly horrible people, not everyone in his family had been through this. There were ex-girlfriends and boyfriends of the Montgomerys that they were still friends with, relationships that had actually ended well. Why he couldn't have that kind of relationship was beyond him, but he wished it right then because he *really* didn't want to deal with this right now.

He *really* didn't want to deal *her* right now.

That linebacker on his shoulder screamed in his ear. *Just one drink.*

The seductive temptress purred in the other. *Just one, baby. Just one.*

Alex gripped the edge of the door, ignoring their words. He wasn't going to fucking drink today damn it. "Why would I invite you in?"

She waved him off and pushed past him. He hadn't been expecting it since this was his apartment and not the home they'd shared so he let her pass. He cursed himself but closed the door so he wouldn't let all the heat out.

"What the hell, Jessica? Why are you here, and why do you think you can just walk right in? We're divorced. You have no claim to anything here."

She looked over her shoulder and gave him a look that spoke otherwise. "This apartment is a bit small for your tastes, isn't it? I thought you'd have gone with a larger home like you had before." Apparently, she was going to ignore his questions.

He breathed in through his nose and fought for control. "You mean the home you sold after you got it in the divorce."

She waved her hand at him. "Memories."

He snorted and put his hands on his hips. "Right, Jessica. Why are you here?"

"Alexander? The door isn't closed all the way..."

He turned on his heel as Tabitha slowly opened the front door he apparently *hadn't* shut all the way in his anger. He held back a curse. She tentatively stuck her head through the crack and froze, her eyes going wide after a moment. "Oh. I didn't realize you had company. Hello, Jessica."

Damn it. He heard the hurt in her voice, the confusion, and he didn't know what to do about it. He didn't know what to do about anything.

His ex-wife moved past him and stared at Tabitha. "You're the secretary, right?"

Fuck. This wasn't going to end well. He pushed past his ex and went to the front door. "She's the administrative assistant, and you know it, Jess. Come in, babe. You're going to get cold."

He hadn't meant to let the word "babe" slip out, and he instantly regretted it. Jess latched on to it, and in turn, Tabitha.

"Babe?"

Tabitha let out a breath and shook her head. "I'll see you later. You're busy."

"Wait, don't go." He moved toward her, but Jess gripped his elbow. He cursed and Tabitha shook her head.

"I'll call you later, okay? Or you call me. I just…I should let you go." She winced as she closed the door behind her, and Alex pinched the bridge of his nose.

If she knew exactly why he and Jessica had gotten the divorce, why he'd told everyone that his ex-wife had left him and not the other way around, or even why things had gone to shit, she wouldn't have had that look on her face.

Of course, now he was truly fucked.

"Get out," he growled. "You have no place here, Jess. You never did."

"But, Alex…"

He turned on his heel. "What the fuck do you want, Jess? You took everything you could from me before. I have *nothing* left. You don't even like me, and I sure as hell don't like you."

Her eyes went razor sharp, and she lifted her chin. "Well, I guess you're done playing nice."

"I was done a long time ago, and we both know it. What do you want?"

"I need money."

He blew out a breath, clenching his fists at his side. "You've got to be kidding me."

Jess waved her hands in the air. "No. I'm not. Do you think I'd come here and lower myself like I am if I didn't need it? I hit a rough patch, and I need a couple thousand to keep going. I figured since we shared something before, you'd want to help me out. After all, I *was* your wife."

"You're right. You *were* my wife. You aren't anymore. If you need money, get a loan. Or better yet, get a fucking job. I don't have anything for you, Jess, and as it turned out, I never did. So get the fuck out."

"Why? So you can play secretary with the redhead?" she said snidely.

He ground his teeth and did what he should have done in the first place. He stomped the last few steps toward the door and swung it open. "Get out, or I'm calling the police. I don't care if it makes a scene. You were always good at scenes anyway."

"Fuck you."

"You already fucked me over quite enough, Jess."

She gave him a dirty look and strode out of his apartment, not caring to look back. She had to be truly desperate to come back to him, or maybe she figured he would roll over as he'd done in the past.

He pressed his forehead to the wood of the door and cursed himself yet again. He needed to call Tabitha and explain. He needed to figure out what the fuck he was doing with her and himself.

He needed a drink.

No. No, he didn't, actually.

He needed to call Steve, and then he'd call Tabitha.

Because he wasn't going to fucking drink.

Jessica didn't have that hold over him anymore. Only he did. And he'd be damned if he let her push him over the edge again. Damned.

CHAPTER NINE

Alexander had called, but she'd been on the phone with her mother at the time. And then Tabby had been too scared to call back. She knew that was a cop out, but she'd needed time to think about what she'd seen, what she'd told him before that, and what they were going to do when they saw each other again.

She was a coward.

When he'd called the second time, she answered, not knowing what she would say, but she hadn't been able to stop herself. The thing was, she trusted him not to drink, trusted in his strength. She just didn't trust in herself enough to *be* enough for him to not go back to Jessica.

He'd loved that woman so much; it had actually hurt to see. They'd looked perfect together, and though she knew there had to be problems since they hadn't stayed married, she didn't know if those problems could be erased over time. Alexander had never spoken about it, and she hadn't been able to ask.

And she hated that her self-doubt reared its ugly head at that.

They hadn't spoken long on the call and had only made sure each other was okay. Though she had a feeling they had both lied when they'd said they were fine. Instead of the lazy weekend she'd envisioned with him, they'd said they'd see each other Monday and had only texted a little since.

She hadn't been able to cut herself off from him completely, and she hadn't wanted to. From the way he texted back just as quickly as she did, perhaps he felt the same way.

Tabby wanted to slam her hand into her planner at the thought.

Since when was this high school, and why did she care about texts and calls and notes as much as she did. She needed to get her head out of her butt and start acting like an adult. Only, acting like an adult was a whole lot harder when there were actually problems in the world.

Instead of banging her head against anything, however, she set about working since her list for the day seemed to be twice as long as usual. It had been quiet that morning since Wes was at a project site and Storm had locked himself in one of the back offices to hunker down with some sketches, but she hadn't minded. The peacefulness had let her think...of course, thinking about Alexander wasn't the best thing for her to be doing right then. The man in question would be in later that afternoon to talk with the twins about what was needed next for the project he was working on and show them what he had come up with. Tabby had already seen some of it when she'd been at his house, and she wasn't quite sure what she was going to do about that since she didn't feign surprise well. She loved the direction he was going, but since no one knew they were together, it was getting awkward.

They needed to somehow let everyone know soon, and she figured Alexander understood that, as well. Just one more complication in an ever-growing complicated mess. That was who they were together.

Between his family, hers, Michael and Angel, Jessica, Alexander's fighting, the attack that had led to Tabby's training...her head spun.

The front door opened, and Tabby looked up as Harry and Marie Montgomery strolled in, worried looks on their faces. When she'd first started at the company, Harry and Marie had been in charge. They'd retired soon after she'd been hired, with Wes and Storm taking over, but these two would always be the couple that had taken a chance on her.

She stood up quickly and made her way to them. "I didn't know you were coming. Is everything okay?" With Harry's cancer scare the previous year, Tabby's mind couldn't help but race. And her face probably showed her concern.

Harry gave her a huge hug. "I'm fine, darling, but I think one of our own needs help."

Marie kissed her cheek and brought Tabby in for a hug, as well. "Austin called to let us know that Alex told him Jessica is back. We're worried."

Tabby's eyes widened. She hadn't known that Alexander had spoken to his family about his ex. That he had, spoke of how rattled he'd been...or maybe how open he was trying to be now. She wasn't sure, and that bothered her. She and Alexander really needed to sit down and talk.

Storm came out of the office just as Wes walked in from the outside. Apparently, it was going to be a full house.

"What's going on?" Storm asked.

"Yeah, is everyone okay?" Wes put in as he took off his jacket.

Marie blew out a breath. "I know we could have called, but I wanted to see Alex for myself. He's supposed to work today, right?"

Tabby nodded. "He should be in soon, actually." She would have known that anyway because of her job, but the fact that he'd texted her that morning to let her know was another matter.

Storm once again gave her a look she chose to ignore. He truly did see too much, and she wasn't ready to be so open about it.

"Jessica is back," Harry grumbled. "I know we don't know why the two of them broke up, but we all saw that their relationship was toxic. But now she's back, and..."

He trailed off, and Tabby wanted to leave. This was a family discussion even if they were at her place of work. This had always been a *family* work environment, and though they'd done their best to make sure she felt part of it, she would always be an outsider in some respects.

"I should let you guys talk," she said softly. "Maybe you guys want to go back to one of the offices? Or I can."

Marie shook her head even as she gripped Tabby's hand. "You're one of us, darling. No secrets. We're worried about Alex, and I know you've been with him now for a bit, so maybe you can talk to us and give us some insight into his state of mind."

She froze. "Uh...huh?"

"She means you've been working with him on the project here so you've had more one-on-one time with him recently," Storm explained, knowing in his gaze once again.

"Oh," she said lamely. "I don't know."

"Oh, honey, I just don't know what to do," Marie explained. "What if he starts drinking again because of her? What if this is all too much? I want to be able to help him, but he doesn't let me in."

Harry put an arm around her shoulders. "We'll figure this out."

"And we have to trust him, right?" Wes put in. "I mean, if we don't, we could lose him."

Storm grumbled something she couldn't understand, and she clasped her hands together in front of her. She honestly thought Alexander was stronger than what they were thinking, but she didn't know the full backstory that the others might. He'd been through a lot over the past year after rehab and hadn't fallen even once. His family had been put through hell, and he'd gone through the good and bad with them and hadn't once faltered. She had to believe in that. The thing was, she figured he could say no to the bottle because he'd been open about it with her, and she trusted that he was trying. But she didn't know if he could say no to Jessica.

And that confused her.

She was making a mess of this, and it was because she hadn't laid it all out and figured out what the hell she was thinking. How could she trust him not to drink, but distrust that he wouldn't leave her for the woman he'd once loved? The *only* woman he'd loved.

But maybe that was because she didn't trust herself.

What a bitch that made her.

"Tabby?" Marie asked. "What do you think?"

"I don't know," she repeated. "I don't really feel comfortable talking about him like this when he's not here." She let out a breath. "And I trust him to do what he needs to do and come to us or anyone else if he feels that he can't handle it."

"At least someone respects my privacy," Alex bit out from behind them.

They all turned on their heels at his voice, and Tabby wanted to curl up and hide and run toward him all at the same moment. Alexander Montgomery confused her like no other.

But she loved him.

She'd come to the realization after she'd told him about Michael and Angel. She might have been in a small form of love with him when she'd gotten to know him before all of this, but she had truly fallen deep; she was head-over-heels in love with him now.

And that scared her more than she was willing to admit.

"We respect your privacy," Marie said as she walked toward him. Her son stood stiff as a board, his eyes fiery, but Marie didn't back down. "If we didn't, I'd have been in your house by now checking to make sure you were safe and healthy. I trust you to make your own decisions, but I'm your mother, and I'm going to worry. And hiding from that and not talking to my children or my husband about the fact that I *was* worried about you is what got us into this mess to begin with."

Tabby's heart hurt, but she didn't move. She could barely breathe as it was; looking at the man she loved standing alone and apart from the whole. He couldn't think like that, though. He was a Montgomery, damn it, and people loved him. *She* loved him.

Marie put her hands on her son's face and forced him to lean down a bit. She wasn't short by any means, but considering her sons were all above six feet tall, Tabby wasn't sure how she'd been able to raise all of them as she had. The woman had a backbone and strength of steel.

"We love you, damn it. And we're worried." A mother's words, a mother's tone.

Tabby's eyes filled, and she forced the tears back. She would not cry now, damn it. Storm put a hand on her shoulder, and while she needed the comfort, she didn't miss the way Alexander's eyes narrowed at the touch.

"I'm not going to drink," he mumbled. He pulled away from Marie's hands but gripped them in his own instead of moving all the way back. "Jessica is back in town because she wanted money. I said no, she got loud. End of story. I know this is going to be hard, but every time something shitty happens around here, you guys don't have to go guns blazing around me as if I'm going to fall off the wagon. I love that you guys are my support system, but I can't be worried that I'm going to worry you guys. It gets too confusing and hard."

"We're always going to worry," Harry put in. "But I'm going to fret about all my kids. I can't help it. Each of you put these gray hairs on my head, and I love every damn one of them and every damn one of you. So know that we're going to worry, but we're also going to trust you." He looked over at Tabby, and she stiffened. "Much like this young lady trusts you."

Alexander met her gaze, and she didn't know what to do, what to say. "Yeah?" he said softly. "You trust me."

"Of course," she said simply, but it wasn't simple at all. "I trust you to ask for help if you need it. And I trust that your support system goes beyond the people in this room. It's not blind trust, it's the fact that you're learning to trust yourself."

She'd said far more than she'd planned to and didn't miss the curious glances everyone sent her way. They had to know there was something going on between her and Alexander by now, but at least they were gracious enough not to mention it. At least...not yet.

When Alexander gave her a soft nod, she relaxed, knowing the worry wasn't over, but they were going to get through this. There was still something going on in the undercurrents around them, but she had to believe in her words.

She'd said she trusted him, and she was going to do everything in her power to make sure she wasn't a liar.

If only she could trust her worth just as much.

****

Later that night, Alex rested his head on the back of his couch as Tabitha made her way back into the living room with two glasses of water in her hands. He hadn't been thirsty, but she'd needed something to do. She'd come straight over after work since he'd texted her, asking her to do so, and he was grateful she'd come. Only he wasn't sure how to begin.

He'd been thrown when he heard her words in the office that morning. Just as thrown as he'd been seeing his family talk about him as if he were a fragile bird. He might have been once, but he was learning to fly again.

Or some shit like that. Griffin was the writer; he just took pictures.

"So...it's been an interesting few days," she began, and he nodded.

"*Interesting* is a good word for it," he put in.

"Do you...do you want to tell me what happened?"

He took her water glass from her hands and set it on the table next to his. Then he turned so they were facing each other on the couch.

"I think that if I'm going to do that, I need to start at the beginning."

She slid her hands into his. "You can tell me," she whispered. "You can tell me anything."

He let out a breath. "I've never told anyone," he said casually, though he was anything but casual. "Somehow, I've made it through countless sessions and talks with people who are trying to help me, and I haven't said the words I probably should have long ago."

"If you're not ready, you don't have to."

Alex met her gaze. "But maybe I have to be ready, or at least pretend to, because I don't think I'm ever going to be ready. Today, my family freaked out because they didn't know what I'd do, and for less than a second this weekend, I wasn't sure what I'd do. But I was stronger than the voices in my head this time, and fuck if I'm going to let the voices win the next time either."

She squeezed his hands.

"I'm an alcoholic," he began. "I will always be an alcoholic, but I'm a recovering one now. At least that's the label they gave me. I haven't had a drink since Decker and Miranda's wedding." The wedding he'd nearly ruined because he'd been so drunk and so far up his own ass that he hadn't thought about the callous words coming out of his mouth or the consequences of his actions.

"I wasn't always like that, though," he continued. "I don't really remember *not* wanting to drink, but I know I used to be normal."

She shook her head. "No one is ever really normal, you know." She winced. "I mean, it's not like you're evil or abnormal for the disease you have."

He ran his free hand over his face. "A disease. People call it that, and I guess that's true. It's something I started myself, but now I can't stop it. Or at least I couldn't stop. Now, I've trained myself to focus on other things and say no to the voices that tell me it's just one drink, just one drop." He shook off the words. "I'm going in circles. Like I said, I need to go to the beginning."

"And I need to not interrupt," she said with a wince.

He leaned forward and gave her a quick kiss, surprising them both. "You're trying, and you're listening, that's all I can ask for." He blew out a hard breath. "Okay, so here it goes." His body felt as if it were falling down into a deep cavern with no end it sight, but his mind wasn't going at the same speed. He couldn't catch up, couldn't breathe. Everything hurt but, at the same time, he felt weightless.

But he had to tell her.

Had to explain.

He needed to tell *someone,* and he knew it could only be her.

He would deal with what that meant later.

"I met Jessica in high school. We weren't friends when we started dating because it happened so fast. She was nicer then, I think. And hell, I was probably nicer, too. We fell hard for each other, and despite everyone saying it was too fast, we got married young. I was still a teenager when I got married for fuck's sake." He shook his head, annoyed with himself for even thinking about that.

"I knew you'd gotten married young," she said softly. "You and Meghan were the first Montgomerys, right?"

He nodded. "And both of us ended up divorced I think before the next set got married." He took a sip of water, his throat parched. "Anyway, though Jess and I fought sometimes like all couples seem to do, we did okay for the first couple of years. We mostly fought about money and how we didn't have a lot of it. And then we fought about the house and school and jobs and all of that crap. But I loved her, so I did everything I could to make sure she was happy. I thought she was doing the same for me...but she wasn't."

And this was where it got hard, where he felt like he was dying every second of every day.

A soft hand slid into his once more, and he centered himself. He could do this with her. Only her.

"A couple of years into our marriage, we both decided we wanted kids. We might have been young, but we were at a place where we were ready. Or, at least I thought we were."

Tabitha's eyes filled, but she blinked the tears back.

And he hadn't even gotten to the hard part yet.

"We got pregnant right away," he croaked. He took another sip of water. He needed to just blurt out the rest of it, or he'd never be able to function. "She miscarried during the second month."

He let out a breath. "At least, that's what she told me," he whispered.

"Oh God," Tabitha breathed.

He couldn't look at her when he spoke next, or he'd break. Instead, he pulled her into his lap so he had something to hold on to, someone who he knew wouldn't let him down. He didn't know why he knew that, but he did. She tucked into him and burrowed in. And that was how he could say what he needed to next.

"Jess was so broken up about it, and I did everything I could to make sure she was as comfortable as possible without showing too much of what I felt. I mean, I was *dying* inside, because damn it, that was our baby. One minute we were planning a nursery, the next, everything had changed. But I didn't say the platitudes that others would have, like how we could keep trying, or that there would always be more babies. That had seemed so callous to me. I started drinking a little here, a little there, to numb some of the pain, but it wasn't that bad yet. Not yet."

He kissed the top of Tabitha's head when he felt tears on his shirt, but she didn't speak. And he was grateful because he wasn't sure he could continue if she did.

"A year later, she came to me wanting to try again. At that point, I felt like I was ready again, and I stopped drinking altogether because I wanted to be a good dad, you know? My dad doesn't really drink except for a beer or two here and there, but while we were trying, I wanted nothing in my system to mess up the baby. It sounds stupid now, but I really wanted to do my part." A pause. "She got pregnant again right away, and we were both so excited. I pampered her and made sure she had everything she needed." He swallowed hard. "She lost the baby a month later."

Tabitha hugged him tightly.

"I started drinking a bit more, but not too much. No one noticed, and I still don't know if that's when my problem really started or if it was later...after..." He trailed off, regaining his strength. "This happened four more times until the last time when she passed out in the living room. I took her to the ER, and that's when everything fell apart around me. You see, I hadn't been home any of the times she'd lost the babies. I'd been working, and that too was another mark against me. I was working, and I'd been too late. But this time, I was there. I was there when the doctor mentioned that the last abortion must have been too much for her, and she needed to go in for an emergency surgery so they could stop the bleeding."

Tears slid down his cheeks now, and Tabitha froze in his hold.

"The whole time we'd been trying to have children, she hadn't been on the same page as me." He let out a breath. "I would have *never* forced her to have a child. I totally believed it was her choice what she did with her body. And if she had come to me and said she wasn't ready, I'd have understood. Hell, I'd have gotten a vasectomy and learned to see a future without children. But we'd gone ten years together, and she hadn't said a word. She was the one who kept coming back to me, kept saying let's try one more time. I had been so scared to hurt her, so scared to lose another part of us, but I hadn't been able to say no to her."

He rubbed his eyes, keeping Tabitha close. "I started drinking more then. Drinking so much I couldn't stop. When Jess came out of surgery, she was angry with me. She put it all on me, and how she kept trying to have children because it was my idea, though it hadn't been. I let her yell at me, let her blame me because I blamed myself, as well. And I kept drinking."

"Oh, Alexander," Tabitha whispered. "I'm so sorry."

"Me, too." He coughed, his throat closing up. "Me, too. I don't know if Jess just liked the attention when she was pregnant, or if she truly kept changing her mind, but it killed me each time she miscarried, and as soon as I learned the truth, I couldn't take it anymore. I kicked her out once she was healthy because I couldn't stand being lied to. But then I was too drunk and too weak to keep my stance, and I let her back in. Then she left me for another guy."

He rubbed his cheek on the top of her head again. The woman in his arms grounded him, and though he was breaking once more over the words he was saying, he didn't want to drink. He wanted to be strong.

For Tabitha. For himself.

For what he'd lost and would never have again.

"I'm pro-choice," he whispered. "I totally believe that it's a woman's right to choose. My mother and sisters have shown me how to be a better man and to understand things like that. But this...this felt different. We were *trying* for kids, and she kept taking them away. I never knew what to think about that. I still don't."

Tabitha moved in his arms again so she was straddling him. When she cupped his face, her gaze met his. "That's on her. Not you. You both went into each time saying that you were trying for children. She lied to you. I don't know what was going on in her mind when she did that, and I hate her for it. I hate that she did this to you. I hate that you started drinking because of it. But you're a stronger man now than you were before. And I trust that no matter what comes next, you're going to fight your hardest against the cravings. I trust, you Alexander." A soft kiss. "I trust you."

He held her close as they rocked together, his world off axis once again.

Yet with Tabitha in his arms, he felt as if he could find his feet, find his balance. And that should have scared him, but it didn't. Not right then, and maybe not again.

CHAPTER TEN

Sometimes, when everything else seemed like it was falling apart around you, going out on a simple date that was anything but simple sounded like the perfect answer.

"Dinner and a movie?" Tabby asked after taking a sip of her coffee. It may be the evening, but she hadn't slept much the night before, and she really needed the caffeine boost.

They were in her kitchen, trying to think about their plans for the night. They'd bought comedy tickets for a downtown show, but neither one of them had felt up to going after everything that had happened the night before.

Alexander played with his water glass as he looked at his phone. "We went to a movie last week, and it was the only one we wanted to see. I don't think anything else came out that was on our radar. Right?" He kept searching, and she set her coffee down so she could slide underneath his arm. She ended up with her back to his chest and his arms wrapped around her as they looked at movie times at his phone.

"This one looks like a buddy cop movie, but it's the third in a franchise, I think," she said when she pointed at one of the bright movie posters on his phone.

He rested his chin on the top of her head, and she held back a sigh. Things were rocky emotionally, but times like these just reminded her that they were an actual couple that was trying to find their way. She still didn't know how it had happened, but somehow, she'd ended up in a serious relationship with Alexander Montgomery, and here she was, in his arms, in her kitchen, as they went over movie times.

"Yeah," he agreed. "And even though I think I saw the first one, I don't remember it enough to have bothered with the second, or to try out the third." He lowered his head to kiss her shoulder, and she held back a shiver. "Plus, you need to see things in order, or you freak out."

She frowned before stomping on his instep. When he grunted, she smiled, though he couldn't see. His self-defense training was helping, apparently. "You like to see movies and read books in order, too."

"But I don't have a spreadsheet of books I own," he countered. "Nor do I have planner stickers to tell me when my next favorite book is coming out."

She turned in his arms so his phone rested in his hands behind her head. She wrapped her arms around his waist and glared. "It's just good thinking to know what books I've bought and what genre they are. Color-coding saves lives, Alexander."

He bit his lip, and she knew he was trying not to laugh at her. When she rolled her eyes and kissed his chest, he sighed. "It's late anyway. Maybe just dinner? I know that's not the most original date, but I'd rather just spend time with you."

And nothing else he could have said would have mattered more.

He wanted to spend time with her.

He wanted *her*.

Never once in her infatuation with him before he'd almost kissed her in his gym did she really think something like this would happen. It was weird how things could change so quickly, and yet not be that quick at all. She loved him, she knew that much. She also knew that it was too early to tell him. He was still shaken over everything he'd told her about Jessica and what he'd gone through. And she knew that he was doing everything he could to remain sober and strong. There was no way she was going to mess with that.

So she would take her time and just love him like she was.

It was all she could do. And with his arms wrapped around her like this, it didn't seem like a bad idea at all.

"I think dinner sounds perfect." She kissed his chest again. "Of course, now we need to decide on a place to go." When he chuckled, she ducked under his arm to look at the time on her stove. "And it's after six, so we need to go now, or we'll end up eating at like eight, and I'm too old for that."

He smacked her bottom at her words, and she held back a moan. The damn man could make her hot with just one touch, and it wasn't fair. Of course, since she could feel the hard ridge of his cock against her hip, she figured she wasn't alone in being in the mood.

"Dinner first," she said with all seriousness. "I'm hungry, and don't tell me you have a special shake for me or something idiotic like that."

His eyes widened, and he threw his head back in laughter. "Has someone actually said that before?

CARRIE ANN RYAN

That their dick would be good enough? I mean, I've made the hungry reference before I've eaten your pussy, but never the dick one."

She rolled her eyes and leaned into him. "Like you haven't thought of that before."

He wrapped his arm around her as they walked toward the car as if they were a couple without a worry in the world. It would never be like that between them, she knew. No matter what, they would always have to deal with the fact that they had pasts that weren't too pretty. But it was something they would contend with, she knew. Because there wasn't another option in her mind, not if she wanted to stay with him.

And she did. She wanted him; wanted to be with him, and wanted him to love her just as she loved him. She'd just have to bide her time and show him what they could have together.

She pushed those thoughts from her mind, however, because they weren't doing her any good at the moment. They ended up eating at their familiar diner instead of somewhere fancy or elegant. They'd been on dates before and had done the nice outfits and linen tablecloth deal. But tonight was all about comfort food and being relaxed. They both truly needed that after the bombshells they'd dropped on one another.

They snuck into a corner booth even though the diner was busier than usual. She ended up sitting right next to Alexander, and he threw an arm around the high back of the seat so she could lean into him.

"I'm oddly craving gravy," Tabby said with a grin. Alexander raised a brow as he looked down at her and shook his head. "What? I want gravy."

"Just gravy? Are you going to order a boat of it and call it a night?"

She snorted and studied the menu. "No, dork. I need a vessel for said gravy. Probably their fried chicken and mashed potatoes. And maybe bread to dip in the gravy, as well. Nothing good for me, and I don't care. Comfort food should be...comfortable."

When he kissed the top of her head, she relaxed into his side. They could do this, she thought, just be normal. Or some semblance of it, at least.

"What are you getting?" she asked.

Alexander flipped the menu to the salad section and frowned. "Probably a grilled chicken salad or something. I've had it before here, but they don't exactly offer it. I have to ask them to not batter the chicken before they put it on."

She nodded, though that ever-present worry came back. She wouldn't say he had an eating problem because she knew he ate healthy and full courses, but he never indulged in anything. It was as if he were truly afraid of another addiction. They were in public, so this wasn't the time to bring it up, but maybe when they got home, she would mention it. She just hoped he didn't hate her for it.

Once again, she pushed those thoughts from her mind and leaned into him as they enjoyed their date. They ate, talked about nothing important, and just...were. And that was the important thing.

By the time they made it back to her place, she was pleasantly stuffed but had room for dessert. She hadn't ordered it at the diner because she had cake in the fridge here, and had particular plans with said cake and the man at her side.

"Can you come with me to the kitchen?" she asked, trying to keep her tone neutral. He frowned and followed her.

"What's up?"

146

Tabby let out a breath, hoping she was doing the right thing. She pulled out the chocolate cake she had in the fridge—the one she'd bought on a whim because she'd had a bad day but hadn't actually eaten yet—as well as two forks from the drawer.

"I want you to have some cake with me."

He frowned, though his eyes were on the fudge decadence and not her. "I already ate dinner."

She let out a breath and set the cake down on the table. "So I'm going to say something, and it's probably out of line, and you can call me on it, but I've been thinking about it a lot anyway."

His shoulders went rigid, but he nodded. "Okay."

She pressed her lips together and stared directly into his eyes. "I worry about you."

He didn't say anything, so she continued.

"I don't think you have an eating problem, just like I don't think you boxing like you do is an issue most times, but I worry they could *become* problems. And I know no one talks about guys and eating issues, but they do happen, and...I'm going in circles."

He shook his head and folded his arms over his chest. "I eat healthy, Tabitha. That doesn't mean I don't eat. Or that I purge it. I eat the right amount for my body type and my activity level. As for the fighting..." He let out a breath. "Other than the fight that you saw, I don't usually go in guns blazing against a guy I can't beat. It's sanctioned, and a way to burn energy and have fun. It's usually safe. I was an idiot that one time, but I'm not usually."

She moved toward him and put her hands on his chest. When he didn't pull away, she counted that as progress. "I know all of that, and I totally believe you. I know I'm way out of line. But I...worry about you."

She'd almost said she loved him and was thankful she'd said something else just then. This totally wasn't the time for that. "I guess it just feels like you're so rigid in some respects because you're scared to go over the line again like you did with alcohol."

His eyes flared. "Go on."

She pressed her lips together, knowing she was screwing this all up. "I...I'm doing this all wrong. You're not doing *anything* wrong, but I wanted you to see that you are strong, Alexander. You're so freaking strong. I know you don't feel like that, but I see you every day, and I see what you can do. I don't want you to not have cake because you're afraid if you have one bite, you'll never stop. I don't want you to fight people you know you can't win because you think you need to punish yourself. I just want you to know that I'm here. Your family is here. And *you're* here. You know the line. You're not going to cross it. You're not going to overindulge. You won't let yourself. But I don't want you to hurt yourself thinking that you *might*."

He was silent for so long, she was afraid she'd ruined it all. Maybe she had. Maybe she was off base and horribly wrong. Maybe he'd walk out the door right now and never come back.

And if she were wrong about what she'd just said, maybe she would deserve that.

When he moved forward and cupped her face, tears sprang up, and she hated herself for it. "How is it you can see into me when no one else can?"

Because I love you.

Of course, she didn't say that.

"Because I care about you," she whispered, knowing that was all she dare reveal.

"I'm careful about what I eat. Careful about what jobs I take. And usually careful about what I do to my body in the ring. I have to be careful, Tabitha. I wasn't careful with myself before, and I fucked it all up."

"You didn't fuck it up on your own."

Warmth mixed with something else she didn't recognize but that looked a lot like disgust filled his gaze. "She didn't make me drink. That's on me. She might have created the circumstances that led me there, but I was the one who picked up the bottle. And the next bottle. And the one after that until I couldn't count them anymore. I can't blame her fully and live with myself. That's how I got out of the bottle, that's how I made it through rehab and this past year."

She slid her hands around his waist, letting him get what he needed to off his chest.

"I know I can have cake or eat a big meal with my family and that I probably should, but I feel like I truly need to be careful. I don't want to find another addiction." His thumb slid along her cheek. "That's why I almost didn't kiss you," he whispered.

Her eyes widened. "What?"

"I knew I could become addicted to you. Not in the same way, and sure as hell not as dangerously as before, but I knew I needed to be *careful*. I don't throw the word addiction around lightly, and that's what scares me."

She didn't know what to say about that or even what to think. "I don't want you to be scared."

"I don't want to be scared either." He took a deep breath, keeping his hands on her face. "I'm careful, Tabitha. Sometimes too careful, I know. I saw the way my family looked at me, or more accurately, did their best to *not* look at me during the family dinner when you dropped your water." He grinned. "Thanks for that, by the way."

"I hated that everyone got silent around you so I acted my normal dorky self."

His hands left her face but went to her hips instead. "I can't promise I'll eat as much as I used to, and I don't think that was healthy anyway, but I'll try not to focus so much on it. I don't know, I guess it just seemed easier to focus on that and the fighting instead of worrying about whether I was going to pick up another drink instead."

Her heart hurt for him, and she still kicked herself for even bringing any of it up. "I don't want you to eat a ton or go crazy. But I also don't want you to stress over it. However, if you feel you need to because it's helping you stay sober...then I guess I'll shut up." She winced. "I don't really know what I'm doing here beyond reading up on it." She paused. "I couldn't help Michael, as you know. But I don't want to fail you, too."

He cursed and brought her close. "Baby, you're not failing me. You're showing me you care. That's a whole hell of a lot better than standing back and watching me fall. And you didn't fail Michael. Sometimes, you have to take care of yourself, too. That's what you did with him, right? When he couldn't help himself anymore?"

She nodded. "I tried. I really did. But I wasn't enough. And it was getting dangerous to have him there because I never knew when he'd yell again or if the yelling would get worse. I tried to help Angel, but since I wasn't her legal guardian, there wasn't anything I could do. And by then, it was too late, and he was gone. I *know* that the situation with him and what's going on between you and me are two completely different things, and even in my mind, I keep them separate, but sometimes they twist just a bit."

He tucked her hair behind her ear. "I get the twisty part. And you're doing great, babe." He kissed her softly, and she melted into him. "So great that I kind of want to eat cake." His gaze darkened. "But only if I can eat it off your breasts."

150

And just like that, all worries about him and what would happen next vanished. The man had a way about him.

"Are you sure you want cake?" she said softly, her voice with just a hint of a rasp. "I don't want to force you to do anything you don't want to."

He winked. "I think I can come up with an idea or two how to work it off."

She smiled then, knowing at least this part of who they were would be okay. As she'd said, there was nothing wrong with what he was doing, other than the fact that she didn't want it to *be* wrong later. She might have gone too far, but so far, he hadn't said as much.

And from the look in his eyes, the two of them would indeed have cake tonight.

And so much more.

The next evening, when she sat with her friends at Hailey's café, all she could think about was cake. Of course, it didn't help that the woman had baked all these delicious goodies and spread them out in front of them all for their girls' night out, but it wasn't exactly that cake on her mind.

Nope, it was all that Montgomery and the way he could use his tongue.

"You're thinking about something dirty," Maya said, pulling Tabby out of her thoughts. "Spill."

Since those dirty thoughts were about Maya's brother, there was no way Tabby was going to spill anything.

"I have no idea what you're talking about," Tabby said before sipping her hot cocoa. Of course, no one at the large table believed her, but whatever. They would all just have to deal.

"She's lying," Miranda said with a grin. "Lying and all sexually sated. I recognize the look."

Tabby kept her eyes off the youngest Montgomery and kept sipping.

"Of course, you know the look," Hailey said as she sat down in the empty seat at the edge of the table. "You have the same damn one."

Miranda beamed. "I really do. Decker wanted to make sure I was all limber and warm before our girls' night."

Everly, who Tabby had brought with her for the first time to girls' night, leaned over and mock-whispered, "Is everyone so open about their sex lives here?"

Holly, Maya's friend as well as Maya's husband's ex-girlfriend, laughed. "Yep. Well, not me, as I'm not getting any at the moment, but yep."

Maya laughed and wrapped her arm around Holly. "Aww, look at you talking about sex and not blushing. I'm corrupting you right on schedule."

Holly put her hands over her face. "I can't believe I just said that." She lowered her hands and glared at Maya. "You're evil, Maya Montgomery-Gallagher."

Maya preened. "Yes, yes I am. And I'm sexually stated as well in case anyone wants to know. Jake and Border also wanted to make sure I was lubed up before the evening started."

Tabby snorted her drink and had to set it down, using the napkins Meghan handed over to wipe up the mess. There was a reason she loved the Montgomerys, and this evening was only part of it.

"Lubed up?" Meghan asked, her brow raised. As the eldest female Montgomery, she was good at playing big sister. "That's the word you're going for?"

Maya shrugged and lifted a shoulder. "What word should I have used?"

"Well, your sister already said sexually sated," Autumn put in. "I would say I'm wrung out." Griffin Montgomery's bride winked. "I got to play secretary again since Griffin wanted...dictation."

Tabby laughed as the Montgomery sisters groaned. "Do the guys think we're talking about knitting or something?"

Maya raised her brow, the ring in it glittering in the light. "Probably. I can't knit since I have to save my hands for tattooing, but I know Holly knits. She made the best blanket ever for Noah."

Holly groaned. "Yes, I knit. I also collect stickers for my planner. I'm one of those people."

Tabby leaned forward, excitement running through her. "What planner do you use? I'm thinking of going with a bullet journal for the next year, but I love my current one as long as I add extra things digitally."

Holly smiled full on. "You're a planner sister?"

Everly groaned. "Oh, God, there are two of them."

Tabby glared at her friend. "You have one, too, you know. Just because you don't add stickers and stamps to it doesn't make it any less a planner."

"I don't own washi," Everly put in. "That keeps me on the sane side of the line."

"What is washi and how can I use it to stay organized?" Meghan asked. "With the new baby, I feel like I'm going in a hundred different directions."

"Amen," Miranda put in.

Tabby pressed her hands together, her eyes bright. "Ladies, I'm going to educate you soon on the wonderfully passionate world of planners."

"*One of us. One of us.*" Everly's voice was deadpan and robotic, and the table broke out into laughter.

"I don't know when we became the girl group that talks planners and babies instead of doing shots at the bar, but I kind of like it," Maya said. "I'm just sad Callie isn't here because she's home with the baby and taking care of Morgan's Man Cold."

Tabby shuddered. "Ugh. Man Colds."

The girls toasted to that.

Autumn smiled and played with her drink. "We're growing up. Though I'm sure the next girls' night will be at the bar since we don't always hang out at Hailey's."

Hailey shrugged. "You guys said it had to be a short night, and I figured we could get our sugar highs here. The guys are all hanging out tonight anyway since I know your parents wanted the babies, right?"

"Yep," Maya said. "I don't know how Mom and Dad are doing it, but with Leif there, they should be fine."

"What about Leif?" Sierra asked as she came out from the restroom. "He just texted to say the babies were sleeping and the other kids put on a movie."

Tabby grinned, loving the fact that the Montgomerys were so close. She was close to her family, of course, but since she didn't live out there, it was a bit different.

"We were just saying that with Leif there, your parents will be fine," Tabby put in and Sierra smiled.

"He's really grown up into such a wonderful young man," Sierra said. "I can't believe I'm about to raise a teenager."

"The hormones, man," Maya put in. "The hormones."

They raised another glass to that and were laughing as the guys walked in. The group of Montgomerys and their friends truly were a sight to behold. All gruff and bearded with ink and smiles. While they were all sexy in their own way, Tabby only wanted to lick up one of them, and he wasn't with the group. She frowned but didn't say anything, not wanting to bring attention to her and Alexander.

"Couldn't stay away?" Maya asked as she shot out of her seat. Both of her men grabbed her and kissed her far too hard for being in public, yet no one seemed to care.

"Nope," Jake said with a grin.

"Actually, he heard there would be cookies so he was the first to suggest we show up after our game," Border put in.

The guys had oddly enough gone bowling because they'd been bored and hadn't been in the mood to go bar hopping. Apparently, they were all getting a bit older and wiser. Or at least older.

Everyone who had someone went to say hello, and soon, everyone had drinks and cake and were mingling like this was what they had planned all along.

Storm walked up to her, an odd expression on his face. "Alex is in the car," he explained. "He had to email one of the clients something, but he should be in soon."

"Okay," Tabby said slowly. She wasn't sure how long she and Alexander were going to keep their relationship a secret, and frankly, she wasn't sure why they were anymore. It had made sense at the beginning when they were working things out, but now they were closer than they were before.

"Everly," Storm said softly. "I didn't know you'd be here."

Now it was Tabby's turn to give Storm a weird look. "You two know each other?" she asked.

Everly shrugged and smiled at Storm. "We've been friends for a while now."

Storm opened his arms, and Everly went into them easily, as if they'd done it a thousand times before. "I was friends with Jackson."

Tabby snapped her fingers. "You're the one who does things around her place?" She turned to Everly. "Why didn't you tell me?"

Her friend shrugged even as she pulled away from Storm. "Because it never came up, honestly. I wasn't hiding it from you. Promise. But between the kids and the shop, my mind is usually on other things."

Another weird expression slid over Storm's face before he looked like he forced himself to smile. "I help a lot of friends who need things done. Though Wes over there claims I only draw, I sometimes actually use my hands, too."

Wes flipped him off even as he kept up his conversation with Griffin and Autumn.

Interesting. Oh so interesting.

But before she could think too much about it, Alexander walked into the shop, his gaze on her. Before she could think of what she should do, he strode right toward her and cupped her face.

He brushed his lips softly along hers, and she smiled. "Hey," he whispered.

"Hey."

The room went silent, and she blushed, aware that everyone was staring at her.

Maya was the first to break the silence by whistling. "It's about goddamn time."

Tabby met Alexander's gaze and grinned as everyone in the room she cared about started to laugh before going about their business. She'd never been so freaking happy in her life, and she had a feeling anyone who could see her knew it.

She had the man she loved in her arms, friends she cared about surrounding her, and cake right behind her on the table.

There wasn't anything else she could have asked for.

At least, she hoped.

EVERLY

O f course, today her faucet would decide to leak and spray not only water but also whatever had been stuck in the garbage disposal on her kitchen tiles. Her home smelled a bit rotten thanks to the broken sink and its contents, and her head throbbed. She might know how to do some minor house repairs because she'd had to learn when Jackson died, but she didn't know what to do with this.

First, she turned off the water for the house because she had no idea what else to do.

Then she needed to call the one person she knew could help her.

She could have called a service, of course, but then Storm would once again get upset with her and get annoyed that she'd wasted money. Not that he ever got angry since the man never really spoke to her anymore. But it was that stern frown thing he did that told her he was *disappointed* in her. God, how she hated that.

But he'd been Jackson's friend, and had somehow turned into her friend, as well.

So she would suck it up and ask for help.

Oh, how she *hated* asking for help.

Nathan and James cried from the living room where they were playing with blocks, and she sighed. No time to waste. Not with the twins crying and her house getting messier by the moment.

She quickly dialed and hoped for the best.

"Everly? What's wrong?" Storm's voice was brisk but caring at the same time. She truly didn't understand the man. He'd been Jackson's friend and not necessarily hers, yet for some reason, Storm had it in his mind that it was his obligation to help Everly. She'd have cut the cord long ago, but the twins needed a man in their life, even if he only showed up to solve problems. Because, of course, Storm would ask what was wrong. She wouldn't be calling if everything were all right.

"So my sink is backed up and leaking all over my kitchen. I'm not sure what to do at this point. I know you're not a plumber, but you probably have more basic skills than I do since this isn't just a clog."

He let out a curse. "Did you shut off the water?"

"Yep." Because she at least knew that. And whenever she had time, she would be picking up a book in her store to figure out how to do these things herself. There was always a way to find things in her books.

"Okay, be there in a bit. Just don't touch anything." He hung up before she could say something snarky at that, and she sighed.

James let out a shriek, and she rushed to the living room to make sure the twins were okay. Her kitchen might be under water and her bills needed to be paid, but the boys came first. Always.

Storm was on her front porch less than twenty minutes later, and he wasn't alone. A slender woman with a toolkit in her hands stood next to him, a smile on her face.

Everly blinked, surprised, but doing her best to not show it. "Oh, hi. Thanks for coming." She took a step back, and Storm and the woman at his side entered her home.

"This is Jillian, by the way. She's a certified plumber and better at this stuff than I am. Sure, I could have probably fixed it, but she can in half the time."

Jillian rolled her eyes but held out her hand to Everly. "Storm and I were out to eat when you called so I figured I'd come with him. This way, your sink will actually be fixed."

Storm glared at Jillian, but there was heat in his eyes that Everly hadn't seen before. Oh. This had to be his girlfriend. She knew that. Knew he'd been seeing someone. It's not like she and Storm were anything more than two people connected by the ghost in the room anyway, but it was weird to see him like this.

"So, can I go into your kitchen?" Jillian asked. There wasn't a hint of curiosity or jealousy in the other woman's eyes at why Storm would rush over to help Everly like this. Either Jillian was a really confident person, or merely confident in her relationship with Storm.

Either way, it shouldn't, and *didn't* matter to Everly.

"It's right around that way," she pointed. "I'll go with you."

"Uncle Storm!" Nathan screamed as he rushed to Storm's legs, James on his tail.

"You're here!" James yelled.

The two of them didn't really have another level when it came to their voices, no matter how hard Everly tried.

"My boys," Everly explained as Jillian smiled at the two little boys running around Storm's legs.

"They're cute," Jillian said. "Really cute." And from what Everly could see, the other woman meant it. She waved at the boys, who shyly ducked behind Storm's legs. "Okay, I guess I'd better get to work."

Everly immediately walked the other woman to the kitchen, aware that her house wasn't a hundred percent. Her in-laws hated that, but there was only so much a single mother, who also happened to be a business owner, could do daily.

"Oh, fun," Jillian said. Everly wasn't sure if the other woman meant that sarcastically or not. "I'm going to get under your sink and get to work. You can go hang with the boys if you want. Or do one of the thousand things I'm sure you have to do."

Everly gave the other woman a curious glance that Jillian must have read.

"I was brought up by a single dad," Jillian explained. "He didn't have a lot of help, so I kind of raised myself in some ways. I know you probably have lists of things to do so I won't keep you. I'll just make sure you have one less thing on your mind."

"Well, thanks," Everly said before shaking herself. "I really, really appreciate it. And if Storm has the boys, then I actually have a minute to finish paying those bills."

Jillian gave a mock shudder. "Bills. Evil."

"Exactly."

Everly was smiling as she passed her boys crawling all over Storm in the living room. Storm winked when he caught her gaze, surprising her, but she waved at them as she made her way to her small office. Was this what it was like to have someone to help you always? To have a partner when things went a little haywire?

She shook her head and sighed before going back through her paperwork. She sent a quick text off to Tabby as well because she'd forgotten the other woman had called to ask a question. Now that Tabby and Alex were officially an item, she saw less of her friend than usual, but honestly, she couldn't blame her.

The Montgomerys had a way of doing that.

"All done," Jillian said, bringing Everly out of her thoughts.

She looked up and blinked. "Really? How long was I working."

Jillian smiled and leaned a hip along the doorframe. "Only twenty minutes. It was a relatively easy install once I figured out what was wrong. I had a spare part in my truck." She met Everly's gaze and seemed to know what was going through her mind. "If you didn't have the part, you wouldn't have been able to fix it yourself. So don't worry that you didn't. Okay?"

Not sure what to say, Everly picked up her checkbook and nodded. "Well, thank you. I truly appreciate it. How much do I owe you?"

Jillian waved her off. "No need. It was easy."

"But you worked and should be paid for it. It doesn't matter if it was easy or not."

"Well, how about we call it a first-time friend's discount," Jillian said after a moment. "I'll charge you next time, but that means you have to call Storm or me to help you." She winked. "I'll drum up business that way."

Everly laughed, slightly confused, as she put down her checkbook. "Okay, I guess. That can work." She didn't go into an explanation of why she had called Storm to begin with, but then again, she wasn't sure why she had.

The women made their way into the kitchen only to find Storm and the boys cleaning up the mess in there. Everly stood motionless in the doorway as Jillian hip-checked Storm to take away the mop from him and put it away. Everly did her best to fight back the tears that threatened. She was so used to doing things on her own, damn it. She couldn't rely on this.

And that was why her voice was probably a little harsher than she'd have liked when she said, "Thanks for coming and helping. Boys, say goodbye to Storm and Jillian."

Storm once again gave her a weird look but hugged the boys goodbye. Jillian gave them a little wave, and soon, Everly found herself alone with the twins once again.

Alone.

She almost texted Tabby so she could talk about what was going on in her head, only she didn't. There was no use. No matter what, it wouldn't make sense, and in the end, Everly would end up alone. Because that was what she was good at.

CHAPTER ELEVEN

Someone pounded on her front door, and Tabby sucked in a deep breath. She'd had a conference call that morning, and was going to be late for work and had no idea who that could be. Alexander had left her early that morning to head to the gym to work out with Brody, and she figured he wouldn't be the one pounding on her door right then.

A sliver of fear slid through her as she remembered the way the former client, Charles, had come into her office with that anger inside him. But this couldn't be him. He didn't know where she lived, and he was still in jail, awaiting his court hearing.

She rolled her shoulders back and looked through the peephole. As soon as she saw who it was, she shrieked and opened the door.

"What are you guys doing here?" She didn't wait for their answers; instead, she flung herself around the first brother she could reach.

Dare stepped back as he held her close and laughed. "We were in the area."

She pulled away and punched him in the shoulder before wiggling away to hug Fox and then Loch. "In the area? Because Denver is so close to Pennsylvania."

Dare grinned. "It's true."

"Yes, we hopped on a plane to make it happen, but see? We're in the area," Fox teased.

Loch just gave her a look that told her it had been the others' idea, and she shook her head. She loved her brothers so freaking much, even if they annoyed her to no end.

"Well, come inside, but be warned, I'm behind on housework so don't go rat to Mom."

She pulled on Fox's hand as she tugged him inside and the other two followed him. Damn, she'd missed them so much. Her parents, too. As much as the Montgomerys had held her close, they weren't her family. She needed to make sure she saw them more than once a year because if she was getting this mushy now, then she was seriously homesick.

"We won't tell her as long as you don't tell her how *our* houses look," Dare put in.

"Speak for yourself," Loch said. "I'm housebroken."

Tabby rolled her eyes and gave each of them hugs again. They let her do it, so that told her they'd missed her, too.

"What are you doing here?" she asked again. "And don't say you were in the area. I want the truth." Her phone alarm buzzed, and she cursed.

"Don't let Mom hear those words come out of your mouth," Fox teased.

She flipped him off as she turned off her alarm, much to the enjoyment of the others. "That's my alarm telling me I need to put on shoes and head to the office. You're lucky I was even here at this point in the morning since I'm usually at work."

Loch shrugged. "We were going to stop by here first before going to Montgomery Inc. Either way, we would have caught you."

She frowned as she slid on her heels and grabbed her bag. "If you would have called, it would have made things easier."

"Then we wouldn't have surprised you," Fox explained. "And from the way you're getting ready, you're actually going to work now?"

She huffed out a breath. "Yes, I have responsibilities. But you guys can follow me if you want to see where I work. Then you can go play tourist or something. Maybe we can pick up lunch together." Her mind was going in a thousand different directions. "Darn it. You know I plan my days, guys. I'm not good at spontaneity like this."

Dare gave her other brothers a look, and she pressed her lips together. Something was off, and she really wanted to know what it was. "We're worried about you."

She blinked. "Why?"

Fox glared at her while Loch folded his arms over his chest, but it was Dare who spoke again. "Let's see, shall we? You're taking self-defense lessons because some guy attacked you at work. You're dating Alex Montgomery, the guy you've had a crush on, and, apparently, you're still out looking for Michael and Angel in the dead of night. Do I have that right?"

Her eyes wide, she set her things down. "How? How could you know all of that?"

"Why the fuck didn't you tell us to begin with?" Fox put in. "Why did we have to hear from others that shit is going on in your life. This is why you should have stayed in Pennsylvania, damn it. That way, we could have looked out for you."

She narrowed her eyes. "You mean overrun my life."

"Well, you seem to be trying to throw yourself in the deep end out here," Dare yelled.

"Stop it," Loch said slowly, his voice low. "Yelling isn't going to solve anything, and she said she can't be late for work. We're not going to add to her problems." He met Tabby's gaze. "We're not. But we *are* worried. First, Marie Montgomery called Mom to talk about how upset she was that you were hurt. Mom was pissed that she didn't hear it from *you*. Dad's pissed too, and hell, so are we. I know you want to be independent out here, and you're an adult, but if a crazed man *hurts* you, then fucking tell us."

She swallowed hard. "I...I didn't want to worry anyone." And she'd been afraid her brothers, and even her parents, would show up like this. She might be in her mid-twenties, but things like this tended to make her family overreact.

"Well, we're worried," Fox bit out.

"Tell us, damn it," Dare cursed. "Don't hide things like that from us. I know you want to do things on your own, but we want to know things like this. We deserve it."

"As for Michael and Angel," Loch continued, "the guy I contacted out here when you first started looking for him filled me in."

She closed her eyes. No matter how far she was away from her family, they always found out everything. She didn't know why she was hiding things.

"And as for Alex..." Dare sighed. "We want to meet the man you're with and make sure he's good enough for you."

"He's not," Fox clipped.

"Excuse me?" Tabby yelled. "What right do you have to say anything like that about him? You don't even know him."

"No one is good enough for you," Fox explained. "He's in recovery? Good. Because it's damn hard to do that, but as for him and you? That's a whole other matter. No one is good enough for my baby sister."

She rolled her eyes and looked at Loch for his say in this, but he just kept silent. As always. She let out a breath. "I need to go to work."

"We'll go with you, then," Dare said quickly. "We're not going to take over your life while we're out here."

She laughed. "Sure, Dare. Whatever you say. And don't you three have jobs? How did you get time off to come out here?"

"We all work our assess off and never take vacations," Fox explained. "It took some effort, but you're worth it, squirt."

She glared again. "Don't call me that in front of Alexander."

"Ooooh," Fox sang. "It's *Alexander*, is it? Let me guess, are you his *Tabitha*?"

She blushed and pushed it. "Shut up, you toad. Now I'm going to be late so let's get moving."

"She *is* his Tabitha," Fox continued to sing as he followed them toward her car and their rental. "Isn't that the most adorable thing you've ever heard?"

"Like cartoon deer and bunnies," Loch said deadpan.

She flipped them off again, waving to the neighbor with her other hand as they called out to her. She was officially becoming the crazy person next door, and she didn't care. She had her bothers to deal with, a job to get to, and a boyfriend to make sure stayed far away before her brothers hurt him or something.

Easy, right?

She groaned.

Nope, not easy at all.

She ended up with Loch in her passenger seat since they decided they didn't want her driving alone. At least, that's how she read it since her brothers were lovingly overprotective. They'd said it was so they were even in the cars and got to spend time with her, and while that was true, it probably wasn't the whole of it. Thankfully, it was Loch and not either of the other two. Dare would have needled her, and Fox would have kept asking her questions while inevitably answering them for her if she wasn't fast enough.

She loved them all the more for it.

Of course, sitting for so long with a quietly disappointed Loch was just as bad as it would have been with either of the other two. Her brothers knew how to push her buttons, even when all they wanted to do was make sure she was loved and protected.

They walked into Montgomery Inc. as a unit, and she almost paused at the door. It hadn't occurred to her that this wouldn't be okay. The office on most days felt like a work branch of the Montgomery family home. One where she'd always been welcome. Her brothers had never been to her home out here for various reasons. It never made sense for them to come out here, considering it was always cheaper and easier for her to fly to them. They'd tried to come out individually before, but work and family things had always been in the way. Her parents had visited and met the Montgomerys. The two older couples had hit it off, and she loved it.

But now, she was bringing her brothers into her place of work with no warning. Sure, her brothers hadn't given her much—or any—warning, but still. She just hoped that she wouldn't get in trouble for it.

Wes and Storm were in the office as she and her brothers walked in, and they looked up at her, surprised. First, she figured because she was *never* late, even after a conference call that she'd held at home because it had to start horribly early. Second, because she had brought three big dudes with her when she hadn't before.

And this after kissing Alexander in public as she had.

Well, as least she was keeping things interesting.

"Wes, Storm, these are my brothers, Dare, Fox, and Loch," she said as she pointed to everyone. "Guys, this is Wes and Storm, the twins that run Montgomery Inc." She didn't know why she pointed out that they were twins other than the fact that she tended to do so. With such a large Montgomery clan, it was easy to forget that Wes and Storm were even more connected than the others.

Storm's eyes widened as Wes came forward, a smile on his face. "Hey, nice to finally meet the three of you." He looked over at Tabby. "Did we know they were coming? I didn't see it on our planner."

She rolled her eyes as her brothers either laughed out loud or chuckled softly. They knew her planner ways, but what they didn't know was that Wes was almost as bad as she was. Almost.

"We wanted to surprise her," Dare explained.

Storm once again shot her a look before saying hello to her brothers. She didn't know why this felt so weird, but it did. It was like two sets of her family finally meeting, and she wasn't sure what she was going to do about it.

"You should take the day off," Wes said. "In fact, you should have just called and let us know."

"We can probably manage without you for a day," Storm said dryly before looking at her desk as the phone rang. "Maybe."

She laughed and went to answer the phone. The guys might be able to handle things without her, but first, she would make sure they had lists so they could actually do it. The guys talked to one another behind her as she jotted down a message. Sure, Wes or Storm could have answered the phone, but she *liked* her job and wanted to do it while she was there.

As she hung up and turned around, Alexander walked into the office and froze, his eyes going as wide as Storm's had. Well, crap. She'd wanted to take a moment to at least text him and give him a head's up. She'd shown him pictures of her brothers so he had to know who the guys were, but it wasn't the same thing as knowing they were there to probably confront him.

"Alex," Dare said, his voice low.

"Dare, right?" Alexander said, his hand out. "Didn't know you'd be here."

"We surprised her," Fox said dryly, shaking Alexander's hand next.

Loch just gave her boyfriend the chin lift thing that Alexander mimicked. This was going well...right? Or not.

"We're also here to make sure her work and home are safe," Loch said finally, turning to Wes and Storm.

The twins narrowed their eyes, but she hoped it wasn't anger at her brothers for daring to comment on what had happened to her.

She let out a breath and moved toward them, hoping to ease the tension. Only Alexander put his arm around her shoulders and cranked up the tension just that much more—at least for the other guys in the room. Just having Alexander's arm around her settled her enough that she could think.

"We added additional security," Storm said after a moment. "Cameras and motion detectors and a few other things."

"Plus, Tabby hasn't been alone in the office since that night," Wes added.

"Good," Dare asked. "Because she wouldn't be working here if that wasn't the case."

That put her back up. "And Alexander is teaching me to fight back, by the way. Because I'm, you know, a fucking adult. And no one, I repeat *no one* is going to push at me. That includes my obnoxious brothers who think they can tell me what to do. Yes, *one* man came into my place of business and acted irrationally, but that's not going to happen again. We've ramped up security like Storm said, but I'll be damned if I let you cage me." She met the gaze of each man in the room. "Any of you."

Her brothers glared at her while the twins gave her nods, yet it was Alexander's gaze that gave her a little more strength. The respect she saw there moved her more than words could say. Not that she'd be saying anything in front of the others right then.

"She's safe," Alexander said after a moment. "Every employee here is. Now, why don't we go get some lunch or something since it's about that time? That'll give you three ample opportunity to grill me like I think you want to."

She coughed and slapped at his rock-hard abs. Working out like he did truly did wonders for him. "Uh...how about we don't let them grill you."

Dare grinned at her. "Oh, I think he has the right of it."

Fox put his hands in his pockets and rocked back on his heels. "Pretty much, little sister. Sorry to tell you, but this is sort of what we do."

She glared at Loch as he shrugged. "Sorry, Tab, it's on our list."

The guys laughed at that, even the freaking Montgomerys, and she wanted to stomp her foot like a toddler. Not only were they going to be all pushy with the man she was dating, but they were making fun of her and lists at the same time.

Family. Seriously.

After she'd made sure Montgomery Inc. would be okay without her for the afternoon, they headed off to a local café she liked. She'd have rather taken them to Taboo, Hailey's café, but she'd been afraid of seeing more Montgomerys and making this...*thing* a little too big. Since Taboo and Montgomery Ink, the family tattoo shop shared a wall, the chances of that happening were too great. It would have been almost inevitable.

They took a large table in the back, and thankfully, she'd been able to sit next to Alexander. Fox had tried to take her seat, but she could bite back when she wanted to.

"So," Alexander started after they'd ordered their meals. "What do you want to know?"

Loch met his gaze, and Tabby put her hand on Alexander's knee. "What do you think we should know?"

"You guys, stop it," she said, exasperated. "This isn't high school, and he's not my freaking prom date. I'm an adult for fuck's sake." They were in the back of the café, and thankfully, there weren't any kids around, or she'd have felt bad for cursing just then. And considering her family, she had a feeling she wouldn't be the only one letting out an f-bomb or two.

"They're your brothers," Alexander said calmly. "If I hadn't been drunk off my ass when Meghan or Miranda were dating, I'd have done the same thing to

173

Luc and Decker. And I was in rehab when Maya started dating Border and Jake, so I wasn't around for that either." He met each of her brother's gazes; just as calm as he had been the entire afternoon. "Is that what you wanted to know? That I'm an alcoholic? Because that's not a secret. I'm always going to be an alcoholic, but I'm not the drunk I was before. I'm not going to let that define me, but it's still part of me. Can't hide that."

Fox let out a curse as Loch nodded, but it was Dare who spoke. "The fact you got help says more about your character than anything else."

"It was my family that took me to rehab," Alexander pointed out. "I wasn't strong enough to go there myself."

"But you were strong enough to stay," Fox said softly.

"Not everyone asks for help," Loch added. "And those people tend to take down others around them."

Tabby felt their gazes on her, and she knew they were talking about Michael. "I told him everything," she said after a moment. "There are no secrets between us." Other than the fact that she loved him, but she wasn't ready to reveal that. Not yet.

Alexander squeezed her hand, and she relaxed slightly. "What else do you need to know? I'm a photographer but you probably already knew that. I do mostly freelance pieces, and I go more journalistic than stock or catalogue. I work for my family when they need me, but I mostly do things on my own because that's how my profession fits in. I have a small apartment but a decent-sized savings. I don't know when I'm going to buy a house because I already did that before and I want to wait until I'm ready before I make that kind of commitment again."

That was news to her, but she merely listened, and he named a few more things about himself that she already knew. He was taking this far better than she was, that much she could say.

"I also do fights if that's going to worry you," he said lastly, and Tabby held back a groan. She wasn't sure how her brothers were going to react.

"Fights?" Loch asked. She wasn't sure if her brother was intrigued or angry about that. She hated that she couldn't read the man like she could the others.

"I started going to a local gym with a couple of friends of mine, so I had something to do with myself other than wallow in self-pity after the divorce and rehab. They have a boxing ring, so I learned how to fight. I mean, I knew a bit of it from high school and stuff, but not as much as I know now. So I do sanctioned fights within my weight class. Nothing seedy or underground like you're probably thinking, but enough that it's a way to blow off steam in a controlled setting. If you're still here when my next bout is, you should come. I actually get Tabitha to come with me."

Her brothers asked more questions about it, and she wanted to bang her head on the table. Of course, men smashing fists into one another would spark curiously in her brothers. They were all so testosterone-filled it was a wonder they could fit through the damn doorways when they walked into a room.

"I've got to say," Dare started as the waitress cleaned up their plates, "I'm surprised you're so open."

She narrowed her eyes at her brother, but he just winked at her. Damn the man.

"I had to learn to be open in rehab and in my meets," Alexander said simply. "I'm learning to be that way with my family, too, but it's easier with strangers than it is with the people you let down." Tabby squeezed his thigh again. She hated that he felt that way, but she'd stand by him as long as it helped.

"I get that," Loch said softly. "I think we're good," he added, looking at Fox and Dare. "Nice to meet you, Alex."

He looked at Tabby, and she raised her chin. "Tab—"

"Don't 'Tab' me, Lochlan Collins. The three of you not only ganged up on me, but my boyfriend, as well. You're lucky we're in public."

"Babe," Alexander whispered. "It's okay."

She glared at him, too. "It most certainly is not." She stood up, her chin still raised. "Now, go pay the check one of you because you owe us. And then I'm going to show you around my city before you go back to your hotel or wherever you're staying. Because you're sure as hell not staying with me. But I still want you to love Denver as much as I do. Now, hop to it, boys. Do *not* keep me waiting. Oh, and I'm going in Alexander's car, and you guys can follow in mine and the rental. No arguing."

She stomped away, ignoring the way the four of them smiled at her as she did so. Damn men and their damn high-handedness. It was a wonder she could love the lot of them.

By the time she and Alexander made it back to her place and the guys had dropped off her car, she was exhausted and stuffed. Her brothers could pack it away when they wanted to, and they'd felt the need to try out a few different places downtown. She'd joined in, and even Alexander had eaten alongside the guys. But now she was filled to the brim with decadent food and ready to burst.

"So..." she began as she toed off her shoes.

Alexander smiled softly at her as he tugged off his coat. "So."

"That was unexpected."

"I like your brothers. If that helps."

She rolled her eyes. "I will never understand guys, but whatever. I'm glad you like them, and no one threw a punch. That has to count for something."

He moved closer, sliding one hand around her waist and the other into her hair. "It counts." He lowered his mouth to hers, and she moaned into him. "Want to go to bed?" he asked, sending shivers down her body.

She smiled softly. "I can't do anything this week." That had been an unwelcome surprise that morning in addition to her brothers and everything else.

He shrugged and kissed her temple. "Then I'll hold you when you sleep. Need a heating pad or something?"

Hell, it was no wonder she loved this man.

"I'm good with just you holding me." More than good, but she was afraid to say it.

He kissed her again. "Let's get some sleep, babe." He pulled her to the back of her house where her bedroom was, and she sighed into him. After the day she'd had, cuddling with him sounded like the perfect way to end the day.

She just hoped it kept up like this because if she had to let him go, she wasn't sure she would be able to.

CHAPTER TWELVE

"Your form is getting better and better."

"Tell me again why we're doing this in my living room and not at the gym?"

Alex grinned. "Because they're setting up for the fight tonight, and I didn't want to miss a lesson. Keep your elbows up." She pouted at him but did as he asked. He had a feeling she only pouted because she knew it made him hard. He imagined those lips around his cock, and his brain went a little haywire.

"Like this?" she asked, her brows furrowed.

It had been a week since her brothers had come to town for two days before heading back to their busy lives. Things were...different now, but definitely better.

She wore a very sexy blue sports bra with crosses in the front that only made him want to bury his face between them and her breasts. Seriously, he loved her tits and couldn't get enough of them, but he held back since he was teaching her how to protect herself. She also had on these black leggings that molded to her body like a second skin. They rose high and covered her belly button but left her mid-drift bare. They also had a blue stripe on the side and around the waist that matched the bra. He loved that she always matched, even when she wasn't trying. That was just his Tabitha.

His Tabitha.

It shocked him how quickly he'd begun to think of her as his...and how dangerous that was. He wasn't sure what would happen next, and that scared him, but he would go into the future with both feet firmly planted on the ground. He didn't have another option.

"You're doing really good, baby," he said honestly.

"Really?" she beamed. "Probably not good enough for me to fight in the ring next to you," she asked with a wink.

He winced. "I don't know if I would want to see you fight another woman like that and end up with a black eye. I might have to hit someone then."

She rolled her eyes. "But it's okay if you do it?"

He sighed. "There's no way for me to win this, is there?"

"Nope," she said with a wide smile. "You're a sexist pig, and I don't know what I'm going to do with you."

He thought about what he could be doing with her right then, and she punched him softly in the gut. "Hey," he grumped. Her punches were getting harder over time.

"You're thinking about sex, and that's not what I meant."

He licked his lips. "Baby, I'm always thinking about sex in some way. I'm a guy."

"Well, I'm a woman, and I think about sex, too. It's amazing how guys tend to forget that."

He moved forward to take her in his arms, and she held up her hands, blocking him. "What? I'm just going to peel those leggings down your legs a little so they frame your butt, then I'm going to fuck you from behind with your legs pressed together so you're all extra tight. What's wrong with that?"

His cock filled at his words, and she let out a slow breath, her cheeks red. "Holy Jesus we need to try that, but not now. I'm sore from this morning."

He winced. "Fuck, I'm sorry. I was too hard on you." They'd had sex in the shower and then at the edge of the bed. He'd gone harder and faster than he had before, and now he'd fucking hurt her.

She immediately went to him and wrapped her arms around him. "Hey, I'm not complaining. But we had sex *three* times this morning, and *three* times last night. It's a record even for us. I just need some time to breathe before I ride you like a cowgirl tonight."

He smiled despite himself and kissed her on the nose. "You want to ride me?"

She nodded. "Yep. I might even wear a little hat."

He laughed and kissed her again. "That sounds like a plan." He let out a breath and rubbed her back. "What do you say about taking a class with me?" He didn't know where that came from, but he went with it.

She pulled back and watched his face. "What kind of class?"

"A self-defense class. I've taken one before, hence why I learned what I did so I could help you. But I think it would be better if you took a formal one. And I wouldn't mind learning more, too. I might be a big guy, but I don't carry a weapon with me when I'm out on the streets working." He shrugged. This was more about her, and he had a feeling they both knew it, but he'd do anything he could to make her safe.

She bit into her lip. "I...I think that would be nice. I didn't do one before because...well...I felt like I wasn't ready. I mean, I probably should have been considering what happened, but for some reason, I only wanted to work with you. Even before you and I started dating. But after working with you and knowing you'll be by my side, I don't know...I just feel stronger. I feel stronger with you."

He let out a breath, his mind whirling. "I'm not used to that, you know." She frowned, and he continued. "I like it, don't get me wrong. But Jess, well, she never let me be, you know? Never let me help her unless it was what she cornered me into. I'm not comparing you, I'm really not, but it's more the fact that I feel like *me* when I'm with you." He hadn't meant to say all of that, but he was glad he had. He didn't want there to be unspoken topics between them, even if he didn't know where this was going. He just knew that if he kept *not* talking about his sobriety or his past with Jess, he'd fuck up things in the end.

Her eyes widened. She was probably pretty damned surprised he'd brought up Jess, but the two of them were doing better about focusing on the now without forgetting the past completely and thus making the same mistakes. At least, he hoped they were.

"I think I know," she said after a moment.

"And since I'm being so open right now, I should probably mention that she called yesterday."

"Seriously?" she asked, her voice heated.

"I didn't take the call, and she didn't leave a message. If she calls again, I don't plan to answer. She honestly doesn't need me or want to even talk to me. She just likes to be the center of attention, and once she realizes she's not going to get that from me, she'll be gone. She doesn't need me," he repeated. "And I don't need her. I don't know if I ever did."

She met his gaze and let out a slow breath. "I need you," she whispered, brushing her lips on his as she rose to her toes.

His body immediately relaxed. "I need you, too."

They hadn't talked about what they were beyond this, and maybe, just maybe, he could be strong enough for them to be more than they were now. Eventually.

Maybe he could find a way to love again, to be that vulnerable.

Because with Tabitha, he could see that happening.

And that scared him more than anything else in his life.

Later, they arrived at the gym, energy ramping through his body at the thought of the upcoming fight. Tabitha stood by his side, leaning into him as he bounced from foot to foot.

"You're wired," she said with a smile.

He winked down at her. "You know it." He leaned down to whisper in her ear. "I'm probably going to be *really* wired tonight."

She elbowed him in the ribs as Wes and Storm strode toward them. "Behave."

"It's like you don't know me," he said with a laugh as the twins stopped in front of them. Hell, he hadn't realized he could have something like this in his life. Between Tabitha at his side and fucking laughing in public as he was, it was as if he were a different person than he'd been before everything happened. From the look in Wes and Storm's eyes, he wasn't alone.

"Hey," Wes said, his face intent. "You said you were okay if we showed up, and Harper gave us the details."

Harper and Brody walked over as Wes spoke, and Harper winced. "Hope that was okay."

Alex nodded, his arm around Tabitha settling him. "I'm glad you're all here," he said quickly. "Seriously."

Storm studied his face. "Are you going to kick this guy's ass? Because I don't really want to spend my free evening here watching you get beat down."

"Hey, be nice," Jillian said as she slid in between Storm and Wes, hip-checking both twins as she did. "Hey, guys. Sorry, I had to take a call, and I forced the guys to head in without me."

Wes scowled. "I still don't think it was a good idea we left you alone out there."

She waved them off, and Alex scowled with the guys. "I wasn't alone. You were watching me the whole time." She waved her finger at Wes. "Even more than Storm was since, apparently, you guys don't trust me to take care of myself."

Alex stiffened as Tabitha did the same. "That's probably my fault," she said softly. "I was attacked in the office a few weeks ago, and the guys are all on edge."

Jillian's eyes widened, and she turned to glare at Storm. "Why didn't you tell me? Fuck." She moved toward Tabitha and held out her hands. "I am so sorry. I just stepped in it big time. Are you okay? Did you talk to someone?"

Tabitha relaxed immediately at his side, and Alex figured out right then why Storm and Jillian were together. She was just that damn good of a person. Alex might not know the ins and outs of what they had going on, but if she cared about Tabitha like she was showing at the moment, he could count her as a friend.

"I'm fine," Tabitha explained. "Really. Alexander over here is teaching me how to take care of myself, and the two of us are going to take a class together, too."

Jillian smiled at him before turning back to Tabitha. "Good! That's great to hear. What class is it? I could always use a refresher if you want another friend to join in."

"We can all go if it's a co-ed thing," Storm put in. "That way, we all know what we're doing."

"Sounds like a plan to me," Wes put in.

"I don't mind joining if you guys want a crowd," Brody added.

"Same here," Harper said.

Alex looked down at Tabitha as she blinked back tears. He knew one of the main reasons she'd been hesitant about doing something like this in the past was because she hadn't felt safe enough. Now, there would be an entire group of people she knew to surround her as she found her footing. He couldn't ask for better friends or family right then.

"I think there's space," she said softly after a moment. "And, yes, I would love if you guys would join."

"That's perfect!" Jillian said, either oblivious or perfectly ignoring the tension. He had a feeling it was the latter, and he was happy for it. "I know most of the self-defense classes are for women, but I love the ones that cater to everyone. Just because you have a penis doesn't mean you're safe."

The guys winced as Tabitha laughed with Jillian. At least she could find that funny.

"I need to go finish getting ready," he said after they'd talked a bit more. "There are two fights before mine, and then I'm up. I want to be prepared."

Tabitha went up on her toes and kissed him full on the mouth in front of everyone. "Win for me. Okay? Don't forget about the hat."

He groaned at that image and waved everyone off as they laughed. They might not know exactly what she was referencing, but he had a feeling they all had a good idea.

Brody and Harper went into the locker room with him since they were gym members and helped him set up. They would be ringside and in his corner during the bout, and Brody had the timeslot right after Alex's. Harper was taking the night off since he had an early morning consultation, but hadn't wanted to miss his two friends in the ring.

As Alex wrapped his hands, he focused on what he had to do that night. As much as he wanted to think about the warm woman he'd be sharing a bed with, he had to put her out of his mind for now. He'd make mistakes if he thought of her and not about what the other guy was doing. His adrenaline ramped up, but not as much as it had when he'd been waiting for the next drink.

And damned if he didn't like it.

He didn't need a drink that night, and he didn't want one. A small part of him still craved one, but it wasn't the main part. Steve, his sponsor, had said time and time again that just thinking that was progress, and Alex was going to hold him to it.

"You ready?" Brody asked, rolling his neck over his shoulders. "This guy likes to use his right more than his left, even though I've heard his trainer say over and over again to watch it. He doesn't listen."

Alex nodded, moving from foot to foot as he kept his body and mind on task. "Yeah, I've seen. This should be fun," he said with a grin.

Harper rolled his eyes, but he saw the humor in them. The man totally agreed, even if he was trying to act all stoic.

"Let's do this," Alex said. With a fist bump to his crew, he made his way out of the dressing room at the sound of his name. This wasn't some late-night pay-per-view boxing match, but it was fun anyway. He didn't want to end up hurting himself so he couldn't work, or end up in the hospital. He just wanted to do something he enjoyed without putting everything he'd worked for at risk. He wasn't sure if he'd fight again or what came next, but first, he had to win this one.

He didn't need the control as he had before, and he wasn't sure if it was because of the passage of time or the woman watching him from the side of the gym.

He had her at his side, and damn it, he knew he could win this.

And when the bell rang, he focused on the other man in the ring in front of him and did what he did best there. The other guy wasn't as in shape as Alex was, and they both knew it. He also relied heavily on using all of his energy up front to try and knock his opponent out, and that wasn't how Alex played.

Alex dodged out of the way of the guy's right hook and used that moment's lapse and exposure of the man's left side to get him right in the ribs. Alex moved again, this time quicker, and got the man in the chin.

His opponent staggered back but kept swinging. Alex dodged all but one of the punches, too slow to get out of reach of them all if he wanted to fight back. He winced when the hit got him in the chin, but blocked the next two strikes.

His energy ramped up, his body moving quickly and doing exactly what he needed it to. When he'd been drinking, that wasn't the case. He'd always been one step behind, and he refused to be that man again.

186

With one last hook, he got his opponent in the chin, and the man went down. He wasn't out completely, but he was down for the count. The referee held up Alex's hand, and he shouted over his mouth guard as the board displayed his name as the winner.

Only one round, and he'd knocked the guy out. Not a bad time at all.

He went to his corner and gulped down the water Harper tossed at him as the others celebrated. He slid through the ropes and made his way to Tabitha. She jumped in his arms, and he hugged her close even with his damn gloves on.

"You won! But oh my god, I don't think I can watch you get hit again."

He laughed and kissed her hard. "I think I'll go out on top, baby. What do you say to that?"

She slid down his sweaty body as he set her on the ground. "I think we should watch Brody kick some ass and then we can go home, and I'll play doctor before I'm a cowgirl."

She'd said the words at a normal tone so the twins, as well as the rest of their crew, heard her, but he knew neither of them cared one bit. He honestly couldn't wait to get to her house and have a taste of her.

She was better than a fight any day.

After Brody had kicked ass in even a shorter time than Alex had, they said their goodbyes and headed back to Tabitha's place. His cock ached, and he wanted to fuck her right there in his car, but he held back.

Mostly because he didn't need a cop to pull them over, but also because he knew he'd end up breaking something either in him or his damn vehicle if he tried that. He wasn't seventeen anymore, and getting it on inside the small interior just wasn't what it used to be.

As soon as they'd closed the door behind them, Tabitha attacked him, her hands roaming over his body and her lips on his in a mesh of lips and teeth. How the fuck had he gotten so lucky?

She pulled back and winked. "You kiss good and fuck better, so I guess that's why I keep you around." She laughed as she said it, and that's when Alex realized he'd said that last part aloud. Hell, he hadn't meant to do that, hadn't meant to reveal too much.

"Glad to know I fuck better than I kiss," he growled, tugging off her clothes as he kissed each piece of bare skin he revealed.

"And you kiss damn good," she moaned.

He rocked his hard cock against her, and they both shivered. "I need to get inside you, but first, I want to eat you out. It's been hours since I had my face between your legs."

She licked her lips. "And it's been hours since I had your cock in my mouth."

Holy hell. He seriously was the luckiest man alive right then. "How about we do both at the same time."

Her eyes darkened. "How have we not done that yet?"

He stripped off his clothes as well so they were both naked, their bodies clinging to one another in her living room as they kissed and touched and groped. "I don't know, but we need to rectify that situation right now."

He picked her up so her pussy lay over his cock as he carried her to the bedroom. She was so wet that she slid over him with each step, and he almost came right then.

"You are so fucking sexy," he breathed as he set her down on the bed. "I could come just looking at you."

She cupped her breasts and licked her lips. With her red hair splayed over the comforter around her, she looked like some seductive temptress he couldn't quite get enough of. "I think I *have* come by just watching you get yourself off that time."

He laughed roughly, fisting his cock. "You had your hands on your pussy when I did that, woman. You were rolling your clit under your fingers and making all those breathy moans you know I like; it's no wonder we both came in minutes."

He lowered his head and took a nipple into his mouth, sliding his tongue over her fingers. "I fucking love your tits. I love that they bounce when I fuck you and jiggle when you walk quickly in those high heels of yours. I want to punch any guy who stares at them, but then I can't blame them because they are truly magnificent."

She arched her back, pinching one nipple while he bit the other. "You've fucked them before, and when you did, I loved tasting the tip of your cock. I don't mind having them this size when they hurt my back after a long day because I know you'll massage them for me when I get home."

He groaned and knelt on the bed, taking her hip in his hand. "Roll on your side. I could ride your face or have you do the same to me, but this way, if my hips move too fast, I won't choke you with my cock."

She rolled her eyes "You've been watching too much porn."

He slapped her ass even as he laid down on his side and slid one of her legs over his neck. Her wet and pink pussy practically called to him. "You're the one that showed me that site you like. You know the one where they spend the first twenty minutes with shots of him eating her out?"

"It was a hint," she said on a laugh before taking his cock between her lips. Holy hell he loved the way she blew him. She was truly perfect for him.

He pushed that thought quickly out of his head and took her hint. When he licked and sucked at her cunt, she rolled her hips into his face, so he used his hands and his mouth on her, loving the way she moved, the way she tasted, the way she made little humming sounds on his cock when he licked her just right. He sucked on his finger before reaching around her hip and spreading her cheeks to play with her ass. They hadn't gone any farther than this, and he wasn't sure they would, but she liked it when he fucked her ass with his finger as he ate her cunt. He happened to like it just as much if not more.

He sucked on her lower lips before flicking her clit over and over again with his tongue. It was hard to think about more than that with her hand on his balls, his cock down her throat, and one of her fingers probing his prostate.

His eyes crossed when she rubbed him just right, and he pulled back, afraid he was going to come.

"I wasn't done yet," she panted as she rolled on her back.

He quickly kissed her before reaching for a condom and sliding it over his length. He squeezed the base of his cock hard so he could last a few minutes longer.

"I'm not that young, and I want you to ride me like you promised before I come again."

She smiled and pushed at his shoulders. He fell back, and before he knew it, she had her hips over him and was sliding down his cock, her teeth biting into her lip.

"You came three times this morning," she teased, rolling her hips.

He clenched his teeth, his hands digging into her hips as she rode him. "No, you did. I only came once. I don't have the recovery time I did when I was a kid." The drinking had done that to him, but he was lasting longer and longer the more he was with her, and they both knew it.

She frowned and lowered herself so her hands were on his shoulders and her hair cascaded around them. "I knew that," she whispered. "I just tend to mix things up when I'm coming out of my mind."

He steadied her hips above him before slowly sliding in and out of her. When her eyes were the ones to cross this time, he smiled.

"Let's make you come again, then, shall we?"

She panted, her nails digging into his skin. "I thought I was going to ride you."

He increased his pace, thrusting in and out of her with abandoned. "Next." Hard thrust. "Time." Harder thrust.

She narrowed her eyes at him and did something with her inner muscles that made him groan. And since he was so fucking close to coming, she took over, riding him like she wanted to.

He honestly couldn't complain, and held on to her, massaging her breasts as she rode him like the cowgirl she wanted to be.

And when they both came, they were panting and sweaty and out of energy, and he hadn't felt better in his whole life. He held her close, his cock still deep inside, as she caught her breath above him. They didn't say a word, and he was glad for that because he wasn't sure what he would say.

He hadn't meant to get this close to anyone again, but Tabitha left him feeling exposed and raw, open to what she could give him and things he wasn't sure he was willing to take. She hadn't been in his plans, and he knew he hadn't been in hers either. He just prayed that whatever came next, he didn't break her in the process. Because Tabitha was worth so much more than that.

So much more.

CHAPTER THIRTEEN

Alex slid his arm over Tabitha's shoulder as they walked up the drive to his parents' house. For some reason, though he'd done the family gatherings numerous times before this, he was nervous as hell. Of course, this was the first time he was bringing Tabitha with him, and the first time since his family found out about the fighting. Though he'd decided to most likely stop doing bouts, he was pretty sure his parents and siblings were still going to be worried about him.

They always worried.

However, Alex had to take it in stride because at least he *had* family at his back when it came to his recovery. He knew a lot of guys from the center who didn't.

"Why am I nervous?" Tabitha asked, echoing his thoughts. "I mean, I've gone to these almost monthly for years now. And yet, I want to bite my nails and hide under that bush. I mean, it took me four tries to find something to wear, and I'm pretty sure this is the outfit I wore two months ago to this thing."

He stopped them both right before they reached the front door and turned toward her, keeping her in his arms. "I'm nervous, too."

She narrowed her eyes as she put her hands on his chest. "You being nervous is only letting me know that I should be nervous."

He kissed the tip of her nose, and she sighed. "We'll be nervous together. But you know my family loves you, right? I mean, my parents are probably going to be bouncing around with glee at the fact that you're even here. So just go with that."

"But now I'm dating their precious baby boy."

He snorted. "I haven't been their *baby* boy in a long time." He lowered his head to take her lips and froze when his mother cleared her throat.

"You'll always be my baby boy, Alex. Sorry to say, but I even call Austin that when I feel like it. It's a mother's prerogative. Now get inside and stop making out with Tabby on the porch. It's cold outside. And Tabby, honey, I love that outfit. You look stunning in it."

He smiled at the woman in his arms, who smiled wide right back, and he relaxed just a little. *I can do this*, he thought. Just one step at a time.

They were apparently the last to arrive, but he didn't mind that. It wasn't their turn to help with the meal, and he hadn't wanted to be in the way. Plus, it had taken Tabitha a while to get ready. Not that he minded since she'd spent the morning wearing nothing but a lacy bra and panties as she went from outfit to outfit. He'd ended up lying on the bed with his hands laced behind his head as he watched her.

Best view of the morning, that was for sure.

When they entered the living room, it was to see a bit of the normal chaos. Somehow, Leif and Cliff were wrangling the younger kids who could walk into some kind of game where the almost-two-year-old Colin would ride his almost-thirteen-year-old brother's back like a horse. Then, nine-year-old Cliff would spin seven-year-old Sasha around the room before the older ones switched and repeated the actions with the younger ones.

Like always, every time he saw his nieces and nephews, he got that little clutch in his belly, but he shook it off. His kids would have been around Cliff or Sasha's age, the youngest Colin's. If things had worked out differently, maybe he'd have been the one with a kid on his back while he pretended to neigh like a horse.

Yet it shamed him that he'd never once done that. He'd seen the rest of his siblings play around with the kids, and yet didn't really remember holding them beyond when Sasha and Cliff had been babies. Of course, he hadn't known everything he knew now at that time, and Leif hadn't been around until a couple of years ago.

But he wasn't sure he had ever held Colin, or the new set of babies that had come into their lives a few months ago when all three of his sisters gave birth within the span of a few weeks.

"What's wrong?" Tabitha whispered.

He leaned down so only she could hear. "I've been a shitty uncle," he said, his voice slightly raw.

She looked up at him, understanding in her eyes. She was the only one who would have the capacity to understand, and he was pretty sure she would be the only one forever. He didn't know if he had the strength to tell his family all that had happened. Some things weren't meant to be shared beyond those closest to him. How Tabitha had become that person over his siblings, he didn't know, but he couldn't afford to look too closely at that right then.

"You can be a better one now," she said softly. She pointed over at the other corner where the other three babies were lying down on their play mats, watchful adult eyes on them. "Go hold your niece or nephew, Alexander."

He let out a breath. "Only if you come with me."

Her eyes brightened. "You're asking me to hold an adorable baby? I think I can manage that." She took her hand in his and led him to where the three youngest were playing. They passed by the other adults in the room as they did, and he nodded his hellos, but Tabitha was on a mission, and they weren't about to stop.

He wasn't sure he had the strength to start again if they did anyway.

Luc looked up from the floor next to the setup of learning mats and grinned. "Come to hang out with the droolers?"

Meghan nudged her husband from her place on the floor next to him. "They only drool a little. And they roll over and can even do other tricks, too." She leaned down and tickled her daughter next to her. "Yes, you do, my Emma darling. You're so smart."

"They're not puppies, baby," Luc drawled.

"But they're adorable," Alex said roughly. "I'll give all of you that, you guys sure know how to make them cute."

Meghan smiled brightly at him before a hesitant look filled her eyes. He hated that he was the cause of that, but how could he blame her? He'd never once held her daughter. It had been too painful, and in the end, his actions had hurt everyone.

"Thanks, Alex."

He let out a breath and tugged on Tabitha's hand as they sat next to the learning mat area. "Do you think..." He cleared his throat. "Do you think I can hold her?"

"Of course," Luc said since it appeared Meghan couldn't quite find the words. Instead, it looked liked his sister was holding back tears.

Alex was aware that the rest of the crowd in the room watched them, but he ignored it. He only had eyes for the baby Luc set in his arms. Since Emma was five months or so, she wasn't the tiny baby she'd been when he first met her, but she was still so fragile.

Alex swallowed hard as the surprisingly heavy weight of his niece latched on to him, her brown eyes wide and curious. Her tiny hands roamed over his face as he put a steadying hand on her back. She had springy black curls on her head that he figured would grow out just like Luc's sisters' and be gorgeous. Her skin wasn't quite as dark as Luc's but was a smooth brown, soft under his fingertips. She was seriously adorable.

"Hey, Emma," he said softly, his voice hoarse.

She blinked up at him, a small smile on her face.

He laughed and looked over at Meghan and Luc. "You're going to have trouble on your hands in the future, I'd say."

Sasha ran to Alex's side and kissed her baby sister on the top of the head. "That's what Daddy says about me."

The adults in the room cracked up, and Alex shifted Emma in his arms so he could hug Sasha close, as well. Meghan was openly crying at this, and Tabitha had Maya's son, Noah, in her arms, making funny faces at the boy as Noah laughed.

This was family, he thought. And he'd almost lost it all because he'd been scared, hurt, and hiding from everyone. He wasn't sure he'd ever be able to tell the others about what had happened with Jess and why he'd fallen as hard as he had, but he could try to come back to them, try to be this new version of Alex who wasn't quite sure who he was but was at least *there*.

He held Emma for a bit longer before holding Noah and Micah in turn. Then he rolled around with Colin and Sasha as Leif and Cliff laughed. His heart ached, his chest too tight as he played, but he did it anyway. Maybe the next time he did this, the next time he took a deep breath and watched his nieces and nephews grow, it wouldn't hurt this much.

Throughout it all, Tabitha was by his side, laughing with him, yet keeping a careful eye on him. Hell, the whole family kept a watchful eye on him, but he knew Tabitha had the only true reason to.

He wasn't sure how she'd given him the strength to do this, to play around and learn to be an uncle again, but he'd take it. He just didn't know what he'd do with the other feelings that came from being with her.

He honestly wasn't sure if he could risk himself by falling in love again.

And he'd be damned if he hurt Tabitha.

Something must have shown on his face because she looked at him oddly before standing up, chewing on her lip. "I'm going make sure your mom is okay with setting up for the meal."

"It's all set, actually," his mom said as she walked toward them. "I seem to be overhearing all of your conversations today," she said with a laugh. "Okay, folks, dinner time," she called out to the rest of the crew. "Everyone take your seats, and thank Autumn and Griffin for helping."

Tabby held out a hand, and Alex took it, careful not to pull her down with him as she helped him up. "You doing okay?"

He leaned down and brushed a kiss along her cheek. "Yeah. Yeah, I am."

She studied his face before taking his hand in hers again and walking with him toward the dining room where the others were finding their seats. If he were honest, it was weird to have Tabitha with him. The last time they were at one of these, he was doing his damnedest not to focus on her, and now they were out in the open as a couple.

He'd only brought one other person in his life to something like this, and Jess had never fit in with the Montgomerys. He wasn't sure she'd ever really tried, even when they'd been in high school, and he'd been a bumbling teenager too happy getting laid to look deeper into the woman he claimed to love.

Alex pushed those thoughts from his mind as he took a seat next to Tabitha. There was no use dwelling on that anymore, not when there was nothing he could do about the past. But maybe he could figure out how to make the present and even the future something he could bear.

They ate together with laughter and inside jokes, and Alex actually joined in with some. He ate just as much as he had been recently, but he didn't make a big deal about it, and neither did anyone else. He just ate until he was full and called it a day. Tabitha had been right in that he'd been too careful, too cognizant. He'd been so afraid of going overboard that he'd ended up stressing himself out over it. And like with anything, he just had to find a balance.

After the meal, the kids went to one of the other rooms to play and watch a movie while the babies napped. That left the adults in the large living room that could barely hold all the Montgomerys and their other halves. It was crazy to think how much they'd grown in the past few years, and yet he knew that once

Storm and Wes found someone they wanted to bring to these things, it would only grow more. Not to mention the fact that there would probably be more babies on the way eventually, as well.

He paused.

When had he started thinking of himself and Tabitha with a future in which she'd always be there with him? He swallowed hard before taking a sip of his water. Hell, he needed to think about something else or he'd stress himself out.

He might as well do what he'd thought about doing for a while now.

Make something right.

He cleared his throat and looked around the room. "Can I talk for a bit?" he asked, his voice hesitant. Tabitha squeezed his hand before moving away slightly to give him space. He didn't know how she knew that he needed that, but he was damn grateful that she understood him so well.

"What is it, honey?" his mother asked as she sat down on the extra-large recliner next to his father.

"You can tell us anything," his dad said.

Alex looked down at his glass and nodded. "I've talked to all of you individually, but not enough. Not enough that it matters; that means it'll stick. I don't know where to start or what to say really, but I figure I should start with what I was saying before this. Or at least what I've been saying to others. Hello, I'm Alex, and I'm an alcoholic."

He took a deep breath and looked at each of his siblings and their spouses in turn.

"I'm not the man I was before the drinking, and I'm sure as hell not the man I was when I drank. I don't know how to apologize for the things I did, for the things I said. I don't know if I should be forgiven for falling out of your lives. I mean, I said horrible things, did horrible things. I wasn't a good person, and I still don't know if I am. I'm just trying to find out if I *can* be. Even throughout the past year, I've been focusing on myself, not really part of the whole, even though I've tried to at least be here."

He let out a shaky breath, and thankfully, everyone kept silent.

"I didn't know how I could fit in, and most days, I still don't. I drank because..." he sighed. "I drank because I needed to forget things. I needed to not feel everything all at once because it was like it was clawing me up inside, waiting to get out, and I couldn't find the strength to deal with it. In some respects, I drank because it was the easiest way out, and at first, I didn't even know I was doing it. A drink here, a beer there. We all do it, so what's the problem? Only I didn't know how to stop. I've watched each of you slowly start to have a beer or a glass of wine around me, and each of you knows when to stop or when you're done. I don't have that filter. I can't stop at one or two. So I can't have any."

"You're fucking stronger than you think," Austin put in. "You may not have been before, and I don't know what happened to make you feel that way, but the man in front of me? That man is fucking strong. That man knows how to ask for help, and to me, that's the bravest and strongest thing you can do."

"Fuck yeah," Decker added.

"Fuck yeah," Maya whispered.

Alex wiped the tears from his face, not caring that his family saw him like this. They'd seen him at his worst, and a few tears wouldn't tarnish that.

"I hurt each and every one of you, I know that. But Miranda and Decker? I'm so fucking sorry I acted out like I did at your wedding. I made a mistake, and I can never make it up to you, never erase what I did."

His baby sister, the only sibling that was younger than him, stood up from her husband's lap and walked over to him. She wrapped her arms around his waist and kissed his chin.

"I love you, Alex. And when I look back at that day, I remember the day I married the man of my dreams, and the day my big brother started to get healthy again. That's all that matters to me."

His body shuddered, and he held her close, leaving a kiss on the top of her head. He looked up and over her at Luc and Meghan and pressed his lips together.

"I hurt you both that day, and I'm sorry about that."

Meghan shook her head. "You're a different person now, honey. I know that."

"And I'd go through that a hundred times more if it meant you came back to us," Luc put in.

"We forgive you," Storm said softly. "But you need to forgive yourself, okay?"

"Because you're one of us, damn it," Wes added. "We're not giving up on you that easily."

Alex squeezed Miranda tightly before letting her go back to Decker. He met Tabitha's gaze and gave her a nod, telling her he would be okay. He had to be okay.

Alex let out a breath. "I hope you don't. Because I'm an alcoholic. I'm going to be an alcoholic today, and I'm going to be one tomorrow, as well. Just like I will be the day after that. But I can promise you I won't take a drink today. And I won't take one tomorrow. That's all I've got." He'd said those words before, but they were the honest truth. He had nothing else to give other than that, and he hoped it would be enough.

The others stood then, taking turns giving him hugs and kisses on the cheek. Even Griffin kissed him smack on the lips with a grin. "We all fuck up, you know, but that's what builds character. Just don't fuck up again."

Alex punched Griffin in the shoulder as Tabitha hugged Alex close. "You're an asshole."

"We're family, man," Griffin explained. "We're all assholes who love each other."

Tabitha laughed in Alex's arms. "I think that should be your Montgomery family motto."

His mother laughed in his father's arms, even as she wiped away tears. "My babies are so eloquent."

His father kissed his wife's temple and winked at the lot of them. "I'll start making the sign for the family room tomorrow. I think a nice cherry would be a good wood for that."

"I'll help," Griffin put in.

"No!"

Alex wasn't sure who'd said it, but it sounded like six or seven of them at once. He threw back his head and laughed as Griffin flipped them all off.

"That was *one* time with the saw," Griffin growled. "One time."

Autumn rubbed her husband's chest. "Any time you have to mention just one time with a saw, baby, is too much."

Alex shook his head and laughed with his family, a heavy weight lifting ever so slightly off his chest.

He could do this, he thought. He could be a Montgomery again.

He looked down at Tabitha. Now, he just had to remember how to be more.

By the time they headed back to her place, he was exhausted. He was not only emotionally wrung out, but he was pretty sure he was bruised in a few places, as well. Austin and Luc had wanted to play a game of touch football so, of course, everyone had joined in. Somehow, Alex had ended up with Maya's elbow under his ribs, and he felt like an old man because of it.

"She really had you down flat, didn't she?" Tabitha teased.

Alex lifted his lip in a snarl. "Shut it, woman."

"What? I can't help it if my team won and your team got their butt's kicked."

"You'll pay for that," he growled and lifted her over his head with his last remaining strength before he set her down on her feet in front of him. "I'd do more, but I'm actually out of breath."

She smiled up at him before wrapping her arms around his neck. "You do look good all sweaty."

He bit down on her jaw lightly. "So do you."

With a sigh, she rested her head on his chest, and he breathed in the scent of her. "I'm so proud of you, you know. Is it any wonder I love you?"

They both froze, and she slowly pulled away from him. His chest pounded, and he blinked. Her eyes were wide as a look of abject horror crossed her face.

He didn't say anything. He didn't know how. Didn't know what. The only other person he'd loved who had told him she loved him back had fucked him over, and he wasn't sure what he should do now. He wasn't the person he was before, the one who loved so openly. And now, he was afraid this never-ending silence was going to kill them both.

He didn't know what to say. Didn't know what to do.

Tabitha was the one to speak first, and he hated himself for it. "I need to shower and get the grime off before bed. I'll be quick."

She dashed off and out of his arms, and he knew he'd made a mistake. Again.

He cared about her, he really did. But he wasn't sure he could ever love again. She deserved so much more than him, and he knew it. He'd known it before he kissed her that first time, and yet, he'd ignored the warnings.

And now it might be too late.

Fuck. Every time he thought he was almost normal, he fucked it up all over again.

Though he probably needed a shower, as well, he didn't join her like he could have just ten minutes prior. Instead, he changed into a pair of sweats and a shirt he'd stashed at her place and slid between the sheets. She came out ten minutes later in a long t-shirt and gave him a smile that didn't quite reach her eyes. When she slid in next to him, they stayed separated for five long seconds before he lifted his arm and she wiggled closer.

He held her to his chest, but they didn't speak, didn't even breathe deeply. She didn't move, didn't hold him back, but burrowed so her head lay over his heart. It took hours, but she finally fell asleep. They might be holding one another, but this was different.

He just prayed it wasn't too different.

Because if it were, he'd lost her before he ever truly understood if he had her.

CHAPTER FOURTEEN

Tabby was an idiot, and there wasn't anything she could say to refute that. She'd said the one thing that neither one of them had been ready for and had made a mess of everything.

Yes, she loved Alexander Montgomery, but sometimes, love wasn't enough.

And from the way he'd reacted to her words, she was afraid this was one of those times.

He hadn't said a word to her the night before, and this morning, he'd kissed her softly on the cheek and whispered that he needed to go back to his house for a change of clothes.

She hadn't had the strength to tell him that she'd washed what he'd left over before and had put it in a drawer. His drawer.

He had a damn drawer in her house, and he couldn't take the fact that she loved him.

How she could be broken and angry all at the same time, she didn't know, but that was sure how she felt.

Of course, last night had probably been one of the worst times to mention that she loved him. It had been too soon into their relationship, and he was too raw from everything that had happened at his family home. The two of them had been faced with bump after bump from their pasts since they'd started dating, and though she'd fallen head over heels for him, that didn't mean he had the time to do the same for her. Logically, she understood that, but it didn't make it any easier for her to stomach.

She looked through her planner blindly as she tried to wake up fully. She needed to finish getting ready and put on her shoes so she could head to work. She wasn't even sure if Alexander would be there today since they hadn't talked about it. They hadn't talked about anything.

She wanted to bash her head against her desk, but thought better of it. Instead, she finished her coffee and found her shoes. She'd just go through her day as if nothing had happened. Once she and Alexander were alone again, they'd have time to think and actually talk to one another.

Honestly, what had she been thinking?

Of him.

Always of him.

But when did she start thinking of herself?

That made her pause, but she pushed it away as soon as she thought about it. Work first. Her life going haywire second.

She slid on her coat and picked up her bag, her mind on what she had to do for the day rather than what had happened the night before. Sure it was there, sitting in the back of her mind, waiting, creeping, just being a nuisance, but she'd deal with it later.

Tabby hummed to herself as she closed the front door behind her and headed to her car. She'd just keep going and swimming like that cartoon fish always said. That's all she could do and stay sane.

The hairs on the back of her neck rose, and she turned on her heel, fists raised, but once again, she was too late. Large hands gripped her upper arms and pulled her back toward her porch.

Charles, the man that had hurt her once before, and the man she'd *thought* was waiting in jail, slammed her into her door. She let out a groan.

"You bitch! It's because of you that they're sending me away. My fucking wife didn't even want to pay for the damn bail, but I made her. She wouldn't have had to do that if it weren't for you. Why couldn't you just do what you were supposed to do in the first place, you whore? I don't see that big man here now, do I? He left you all alone, and that's your fucking fault, too probably."

He'd been watching her? For how long?

Her mind was slow to catch up, but the rage that had been building inside of her finally broke free. When Charles released one arm to raise his fist at her, she used what Alexander had taught her and did the one thing she hadn't truly been able to do before.

She fought *back*.

She kicked the man right in the balls with all of her strength and used her newly free hand to push at him. Charles fell back, reaching for his crotch as he cried out, and she tried to slide out of his hold. Only she wasn't quite fast enough, and he gripped her arm. The momentum pulled her down onto the icy stone step, and she cried out when her arm hit at the wrong angle. Charles wrenched it during his fall, as well, and she felt the bone snap inside her lower arm.

Pain made her dizzy, and she rolled away, clutching her arm to her chest. She'd also hit her face on the sidewalk on the way down, but her arm hurt worse. Her legs could work, though, and she did what she'd promised to do.

She ran.

She left her bag and phone behind, afraid that she'd waste too much time and the man would hurt her worse.

Before she'd made it to her neighbor's house to knock frantically for help, however, the older man who lived there threw open the door and pulled her inside.

"Get inside," he barked, his phone to his ear. "Yeah, get here now," he yelled into the phone. "The guy is on the ground, but I don't know how long he'll stay down. I have Tabby in my house, but send an ambulance."

Joe, the neighbor, looked down at her and cursed. "Sit down right here on the bench, darling. They'll come soon and take care of you. I won't let that fucker hurt you."

Never in her life had she heard her older neighbor curse, and that sent a shock through her, one that finally let the tears fall and the pain come full force. She sank down on the bench and tried to breathe, but she couldn't.

Spots danced along her vision, and bile filled her throat. She was pretty sure she had a concussion, and she should probably stay alert. Only her eyes were too heavy.

The last thing she heard was Joe telling her to stay awake.

But it was too hard.

Everything was just too hard.

At least she'd fought back.

That was the last thought she had before she fell fully on the bench, the pain too much for her to stay conscious.

****

Alex slammed the door open and ran into the waiting room, Storm on his heels. He couldn't fucking believe he'd left his damn phone at Tabitha's. He'd never hooked up the landline in his apartment so he'd been cut off from the world until Storm had practically broken down his door to get inside.

His chest felt like there was a vice around it, squeezing until he couldn't breathe, but he couldn't focus on that. Not when Tabitha was hurt and alone.

Damn it.

Why the fuck hadn't he been there?

Oh, right, because he'd been too chickenshit to deal with his feelings, so he'd left her there for some asshole to find. The fucker had apparently been out on bail for a full day and had somehow found out where Tabitha lived. He'd attacked her when she was all alone, and now Alex would never forgive himself.

"Slow down," Storm muttered from Alex's side. His brother was moving just as fast as he was so he could stuff it. "Security will take you out of here if you make a scene." He cursed. "Our family has been in this fucking emergency room too many times to count. Or at least one just like it since, apparently, we keep ending up here."

Alex snarled. "Tabitha shouldn't be in here at all. I should have been there to protect her."

Storm tugged on his arm and pulled him to a corner. Alex raged but didn't fight back. Storm was right about security, and he couldn't afford to get kicked out. Not when Tabitha was so close.

"She fought back. You heard me say that right? The cops said she only got hurt because the fucker grabbed her at the last second and there was a patch of ice. She'd have been fine if she hadn't fallen. But she fought back and kicked the guy so hard in the nuts, she actually ruptured a testicle."

Alex held back a wince at that but felt no pity. "She should have ripped his dick off."

"If she'd had more time, she probably would have. But she did the thing you taught her and got away. She *ran.* That's the first priority, right? She ran and got help. If she hadn't slipped, and if that step hadn't been there, she would have been fine. She fought back, Alex. You helped her. Remember that, okay?"

Alex let out a breath, his stomach turning. This was all too much, and he couldn't focus. Before this, he would have gone straight for a drink to mask the emotions, but he couldn't. He *couldn't.* The fact that he'd thought about it at all though told him how close to the edge he was."

Storm met his gaze and cursed. "Hell. What can I do? Do you need me to call your sponsor? Can you handle this, Alex? Because you can't go in there with your fists ready to hit something and break down in front of her. She needs you to be strong. Can you do that?"

He wasn't sure what he could do, and it must have shown on his face.

"Damn it. Tabby needs you, bro. But she needs you healthy. What can I do?" Storm's voice broke, and Alex knew that was the last straw.

His family always did *everything* they could for him, and yet he kept fucking up. He was never enough.

"I need...I need to see her." He paused. "Then I need to call Steve."

Storm nodded. "Okay, then. Let's do this."

The other Montgomerys had already shown up, but Alex moved past them, ignoring their questions and looks of worry. He couldn't handle them right then, and he knew it.

"Only one person at a time," the nurse said. "Are you Alexander? She's been asking for you."

Another punch to the gut.

He nodded. "That's me." His voice was like rough gravel, but the nurse didn't say anything. She just led him back to a small room where the only woman he thought he could love lay on a bed, her face pale and her arm tucked close to her.

"Tabitha."

A broken breath.

"Hi."

A small hollowness.

The nurse left them alone, and he went to her side, his hands shaking. He couldn't touch her. She was so fucking fragile, and he was wired. What if he hurt her again because he couldn't control himself?

A cut marred her forehead, and bruises dotted the side of her face. She had a splint around her wrist, and her teeth were digging into her bottom lip.

"I'm so fucking sorry."

She met his gaze. There were no tears there, and he wasn't sure if that was good or bad.

"You shouldn't be. You didn't put me here. If anything, you made sure it wasn't worse."

He bit off a growl. He couldn't imagine her worse.

"You need to go talk to Steve," she said calmly. "You're shaking, baby. And I don't like to see you in pain."

He let out a hollow laugh. "You're the one in the hospital. You're the one with a splint on your arm and a bruise on your face. I'm fine."

She shook her head and winced. "You're not."

He stayed silent.

"I'm the one with a concussion and a cast to come. The break was clean so no surgery, thankfully. Apparently, I take enough calcium that it didn't shatter like it could have. They might keep me for observation overnight, but when they let me go home, your parents are going to take me to their place to watch me. You mom wouldn't hear another answer." She closed her eyes a moment before opening them to meet his gaze. "You need to go, baby. You need to make sure you can handle this. You need to go because I don't want to be the reason you break."

"Tabitha."

"I can't be that reason, Alexander. I can't."

He leaned down and brushed a kiss across her lips. "I...I'm so fucking sorry. I'll be back, okay? I won't let you down."

She gave him a small smile. "Go."

He felt like he was the one shattering inside, but he left like she'd asked. He passed his family, ignoring their questions, their glares, and went out to the parking lot. Storm followed him silently, and he was grateful. His brother had driven him here, after all.

"I need to make a call," Alex said, his voice breaking.

"Where am I taking you?" Storm asked.

"I don't know yet."

He didn't know anything.

He called Steve right away, and the man told him to meet him at the center. Storm drove him there silently. His brother didn't judge, didn't glare, just took care of him.

One day, Alex wouldn't need this, but he didn't know when that day would be. He hated this part of himself, but he knew this was a part that would never go away.

"You can come in if you want," he said once Storm had pulled up into the parking lot. "I don't mind if you're there."

Storm's hands squeezed the steering wheel. "Not this time. Get the help you need. Find what you need. Then come back out here because Tabby needs you, too."

He nodded, but he wasn't sure that was the truth. He didn't think Tabitha needed him at all. And why should she? She couldn't count on him when it mattered, so what other option did she have?

Steve had two cups of coffee in his hands when Alex showed up. "Just got here, but I picked up coffee on the way. So, first off. Did you have a drink?"

"No."

"Good."

"I didn't want one," Alex put in. "Not like before. It was just a quick flash of memory when I was at the hospital before I got to her, and I was afraid it would be too much. I fucked up, Steve. I really fucked up."

"Alex, you're going to fuck up. We all fuck up. Even the people who haven't tried to drink themselves to death will fuck up. But you can be strong again. Hell, you're strong now. You came to me for help because you knew I'd be here, and I'm the comfortable one to ask. But I saw your brother drop you off. You can have him, too if you need him, I would think. You have a big family that I know you love, and who I know stood behind you through it all. You can lean on them. You can lean on your woman, too. You can lean on me. But you don't need to lean on booze. I can promise you that."

They sat there and talked for over an hour before Storm walked in. He nodded at them both before taking a seat against the wall. Another hour passed, and Alex knew he'd be okay, at least for now.

The thing was, he could have made it by Tabitha's side. He knew that much. Only he hadn't wanted to hurt her again. That was something he'd have to deal with once he saw her. Because he couldn't keep running away every time things got hard. He'd once run to the bottle, but he couldn't justify running at all anymore.

When they were through, Storm drove him to Tabitha's house instead of his own. "When you were in there, Mom called to tell me they're taking her home with them," he explained. "She said you had a key to get your phone. Right?"

Alex nodded. "I'll text her to see if she wants me there."

"Tab? Why wouldn't she want you there?"

"I left, Storm. She told me to go, and I did. I shouldn't have."

Storm shook his head as he pulled up to Tabitha's house. The police had come and gone, apparently, and he was allowed in, but her car was still in the driveway. Had it only been that morning that he'd been there, holding her in his arms and unsure what to do?

He needed to see her, damn it. He just hoped she wanted to see him.

As soon as he got his phone, he sent her a text to make sure she was okay.

I'm okay. Going to sleep soon though your Mom will wake me up in an hour to check on me.

He let out a breath and replied back. *Want me to come?*

Her response took longer than he'd wanted. *Not today. I need some space to heal. And I think you do, too.*

He blinked away the sudden stinging in his eyes and nodded though she couldn't see. *Let met know if you need anything. Thinking of you, baby.*

Same here.

He stuck his phone in his pocket and slid into Storm's car. "Take me home."

Storm looked at him with a frown on his face. "Seriously? You're not going over there."

"She said she needs some space."

"Fuck, man. I'm sorry."

"Not as sorry as I am."

He'd fucked this up, and he wasn't sure what to do about it. He'd give her the space she needed, though, because she deserved that much. She deserved so much more.

Could he love her?

Hell *did* he love her?

Was love this never-ending ache for a person he wasn't sure he could fully live without? Because if that was love, then he fucking felt it for her. He just didn't know if he was strong enough to survive it.

Because Tabitha deserved more than a broken man who couldn't stand by her side.

So he'd wait for her to be ready.

And when that time came, he knew if he didn't live up to what he needed to be, he'd lose her forever.

And he'd deserve every ache and pain that came along with it.

CHAPTER FIFTEEN

Tabby wanted to hurl her phone across the room, but she didn't think that would help anything. It had been three days since she'd come to stay with the Montgomerys. She could have gone home after the first day, but Marie could be persuasive when she wanted to be.

And it probably wasn't lost on the older Montgomery that her son hadn't been by to visit Tabby once.

Oh, he'd tried, but Tabby had warned him off. She'd been honest when she'd said she needed space, even when it hurt her to say it. She would do *anything* for that man, even stay away because she loved him.

Because she'd seen what happened to someone when she pushed too hard like with Michael, and she wasn't about to do that again with Alexander. If he couldn't be the person he needed to be with her, then she couldn't be with him.

He needed more than that.

She needed more than that.

Over the past three days, they had exchanged multiple texts but no calls. They were truly giving each other space, but to what end? She would *never* blame him for what had happened, especially considering what he'd taught her had helped her survive. Just as she would *never* blame him for needing to see Steve.

But she might blame him a little if he couldn't love her because he was too afraid.

She wasn't strong enough to deny that.

The two of them had fallen into their relationship and had progressed far too quickly for where they'd both come from. They had so much baggage between them it wasn't even funny, so it shouldn't have surprised her that they were having trouble now.

But since they'd moved that fast, they each had to face the consequences.

Her phone buzzed, and she frowned, wondering if it would be Alexander calling her. Instead, the screen read Loch's name and she answered.

"Hey, you," she said, putting false cheer into her voice.

"Hey back. How you feeling? Your head okay?"

She'd told her family what had happened as soon as she'd gotten to the Montgomerys, and after Alexander had texted the first time. She knew she'd been stupid in not telling them the first time it had happened, so she wasn't about to make the same mistake. As it was, the Montgomerys and her brothers had gotten together to add new security to her house.

She let them do it because it not only made them feel better, but it also made her feel a little safer. She'd been attacked twice by the same man, and the judge was going to make sure it didn't happen a third time. But with the new security that her parents, as well as Marie and Harry, had assured her wouldn't be overboard, she'd have that extra layer to help her sleep at night.

"I'm okay, actually. My arm aches a bit but not as bad as before. The doctor said I could go back to work after the weekend."

"Hmm."

She rolled her eyes, even though he couldn't see. "I'm fine, you big brute."

"If you're so fine, why did Storm call to tell me that you haven't seen Alex."

She closed her eyes and groaned. "How many big brothers do I need?"

"Well, apparently, all of us together aren't enough since you're in pain, baby sister."

"If you called to talk about my relationship with Alexander, I'm going to hang up now. The two of us will figure out what we're doing when we're ready. Alone."

"Hmm."

"Loch."

"I actually called to talk about something else, not that. But I still don't like seeing you hurting, Tab."

She played with a stray thread on the comforter. "I'm okay."

He sighed into the phone, and she almost sighed with him. "They found Michael, Tab."

She sat up, ignoring the twinge in her arm. "What?"

"He's sober, apparently. He got a job, and Angel is in school. They moved out of Denver a month ago and live in Cheyenne now. They're doing okay according to my contact." He paused. "You don't need to look for them anymore, little sis. He's doing okay. You need to be okay, too."

She blinked a few times, trying to collect her thoughts. For the past four years, she'd spent countless hours worrying about the man that had been part of her life, and the child she'd loved. Only she wasn't enough for them. She thought she'd lost them forever in the worst way possible, and had blamed herself for standing up to Michael when he'd been too much.

But if he was sober now, and Angel was in school...then it was all over.

For her, at least.

They were going to be okay, at least from the looks of it.

Maybe it was time for her to be okay, too.

"Thanks for letting me know."

"Damn it, Tab. Tell me what you're thinking. I can't tell over the phone."

She sniffed, and he cursed. "I'm really okay. I know I keep saying that word, but it's the only thing I can think of. I searched for them for so long because I thought I had to help them. But if they're doing what they can on their own and doing it well, then I guess I don't need to keep looking. They aren't here anymore."

"No, they aren't, baby sister. But you're there. And so is that man you love."

She froze. "I never told you I loved him."

"We all saw it in your face the moment we looked at you. I don't know how he missed it."

"He wasn't ready to see," she whispered.

"Well, he'd better damn well get ready, or I will come back there and kick his ass. You got me?"

She smiled at her brother's words and laughed, knowing she wouldn't technically ever be alone. "I got you, Loch."

The two of them talked for another few minutes before saying goodbye. She let herself collect her thoughts for a bit longer before getting up and heading downstairs. Today, she was going home, and though she figured the Montgomerys might want her to stay, it was time.

It was past time.

"I've already packed the car, hon," Harry said with a wink. "I knew you'd want to fly the coop eventually."

Tabby smiled. God, she loved this family so freaking much. She hugged him hard and sighed at how much he reminded her of his son. "Thank you for taking care of me."

"Always, Tabby. Always."

Marie hugged her next, and Tabby blinked back tears. "No matter what, baby girl, you're one of ours. Okay?"

Damn it, this family was going to kill her, and she couldn't help but want to keep them close. They helped her gather her remaining things and headed over to her place. She sat in the back, her gaze on the passing road as she tried to think about what she would do next. She needed to call Alexander, she figured. She needed to call *and* see him. She wasn't sure what would happen after that, but the time for giving each other space was over.

When they pulled up in front of her house, however, it seemed she wasn't the only one who had been thinking that.

"I hope it's okay that I called him," Harry said softly. "I figured he could help me get everything out of the car. I'm an old man, you see."

She rolled her eyes and leaned forward to kiss his cheek. "You're not that old, mister."

He grinned and got out of the car first, followed by Marie, who looked like she was holding back a smile, as well. You seriously couldn't get much past a Montgomery, it seemed. And the family sure knew how to meddle—hopefully in the best of ways.

"Tabitha."

She looked over at him and held back a sigh. She'd missed him so freaking much. "Hi."

She didn't know what else to say. Three days of not seeing him, of not hearing his voice, had been too much, and yet she didn't know what to say now.

"We're just going to put her things in the house," Harry put in. "I take it you left the door open, son?"

"Yep," Alexander answered, his gaze only for her.

She frowned and looked over at the older couple. "I thought you wanted Alexander to get the things out of the car, old man?"

Marie laughed. "Shut it and stop thinking too hard about our lies, young lady. We will see you at work or at a family dinner soon." They dropped off her things and left without another word.

Alexander stuffed his hands in his pockets and didn't say anything as his parents drove off. "You're cold."

She blinked up at him. "What?"

He smiled but it didn't reach his eyes. "You're cold, babe. We're both shivering out here because we don't know what to say. Let's go inside and try to actually talk in there."

She snorted but agreed, and soon they were in her living room with their coats off, still as silent as before.

"I'm sorry for pushing you away," she blurted.

Alexander shook his head before reaching out and taking the hand that peeked out of a cast. "No, I'm the sorry one. I'm the one who left. Yeah, you asked, but I still left. I needed a minute to make sure I was steady before I could be the rock you needed. Then when the time came, I stayed away longer than I should have because I didn't know if you wanted me to come back."

She shook her head. "I wanted you. I still want you." She was breaking again. Open. Raw. Shattering. He cupped her face and brushed the tears from her cheeks with his thumbs. "I wanted you, too. And yeah, I still want you. I also stayed away because I needed to understand what I was feeling. You see, I was so fucking scared about loving someone again that I didn't realize what I was feeling at all. I buried my head in the sand and almost lost you because of it."

Her heart shuddered, and her breath quickened. "You haven't lost me, Alexander. Not yet."

He let out a breath. "I was afraid to love you because I was afraid to need you too much. The thing is, that's not something I can control. I need you, Tabitha. I need you with every ounce of my being. Not because I'm not strong enough without you, but because I'm stronger with you. I'm a better man with you in my life, and I want to be the man who loves you. I *am* the man who loves you. You ripped open a part of me I didn't know had scarred over so deeply that I almost lost it. You left me raw, exposed, and *yours*. All of that might sound like I hate it, but it's just the opposite. I don't have that burden inside me anymore, that ache that told me I had to run and hide from anything important. I fucking love you, Tabitha. I love you with everything I am, and I should have loved you far longer than this. I wish to hell that I'd had years with you before this; that I hadn't wasted my time drowning myself in pain and self-pity. But I know we can't go back, we can only move forward. I love you, Tabitha. I love you so fucking much."

Tears flowed freely, and she reached up to kiss him hard on the lips. "You are...you are so much more than your past. Just like I'm so much more than mine. I love you, Alexander. I've loved you for longer than I should have, but I love you more with each passing day. You broke something open in me, too, but you're right, it's the good kind of break. It's a break that's going to let us tangle in each other and be who we need to be, rather than the outcome of past decisions that aren't who we are anymore."

He kissed her again, and she sighed into him. "I'm so glad you got that. Griffin is the one who's good with words. I feel like I'm just throwing things out there at this point, but no matter what, I want you to know that I love you. I want to be with you, Tabitha. I want to learn to be who we are now, by your side. And watch you smile every morning. I want you in our bed, not mine, not yours, but *ours*. I want you in my life, and I want you to be...just I want you to be. Just like I want to be."

She kissed his chest, his chin, his cheeks, then his lips. "I want to be, too. And I believe in you, baby. I believe in you so much."

"I got you something," he whispered, and moved back from her to pick up a rectangular box.

She wiped her face and took it from him. "What would you have done if I'd told you to leave?"

He shrugged and bit into his lip. "I'd have left the box for you to find and tried to persuade you. I'm not giving up on you easily."

"I'm not giving up on you either." She lifted the lid from the box and let out a tiny squeak.

Alexander didn't say anything. Inside was a delicate, handmade wooden frame that held a black and white photo. It was the photo he'd taken of her in the office, with her head down and her lips curving into a small, shy smile. She remembered how much she'd wanted to hide from him when he'd taken that photo, afraid he'd see too much.

And she knew now that she'd had a reason to be worried.

Her love for him resonated through the photo in perfect harmony. Yet she could feel the love of the photographer, *her* photographer just as much.

But that wasn't why she'd made that sound.

Nestled inside a small ledge built into the frame was a white gold ring with a single solitaire shining on top.

She set the box down on the table with shaking hands and held the ring between her thumb and finger with one hand and the frame in the other.

"Alexander?" she breathed.

She looked down at him on one knee and almost fainted right then.

"I know it's early, and I know we should wait, and we will if we want to, but I wanted you to know that I love you and I want you to be my wife. I want to marry you, want to be your husband. I want you to be a damn Montgomery once and for all, and I want to look into our future together knowing we can be anything, do anything, and live through anything as long as we have each other."

She sniffed and went to her knees in front of him, setting the picture on the ground beside them. "Yes," she whispered. "Yes to all of that. Yes, yes, yes."

A single tear fell down his cheek and she leaned forward to kiss it away. He captured her lips in an achingly sweet kiss before pulling back and sliding the ring on her finger.

"I'm going to be a Montgomery," she said after a moment, and they both laughed.

"I honestly didn't know if that was going to be a pro or a con for you," Alexander said with another laugh.

"A pro," she answered. "Totally a pro."

And then she leaned forward and kissed the hell out of her fiancé, Alexander Montgomery. Because yeah, she'd be a Montgomery, after all, it just took her falling in love with the one man most thought she shouldn't to make that happen.

And that sounded like the end of a perfect plan to her.

The End

Coming Next in the Montgomery Ink World:
Two novellas where secret side characters find their happy ever afters.
Then Storm finally finds his other half...in the one woman he shouldn't.

A Note from Carrie Ann

Thank you so much for reading **INK EXPOSED**. I do hope if you liked this story, that you would please leave a review. Not only does a review spread the word to other readers, they let us authors know if you'd like to see more stories like this from us. I love hearing from readers and talking to them when I can. If you want to make sure you know what's coming next from me, you can sign up for my newsletter at www.CarrieAnnRyan.com; follow me on twitter at @CarrieAnnRyan, or like my Facebook page. I also have a Facebook Fan Club where we have trivia, chats, and other goodies. You guys are the reason I get to do what I do and I thank you.

Make sure you're signed up for my MAILING LIST so you can know when the next releases are available as well as find giveaways and FREE READS.

The Montgomery Ink series is an on going series. I hope you get a chance to catch up! Storm and Everly's book is next in INKED EXPRESSIONS. These two surprised me within this book and now I'm chomping at the bit to write their book..

Before their book, however, I have two novellas releasing in 2017. The first is Brody and Holly's story called ADORING INK and releases in Jan 2017 as part of 1001 Dark Nights. Then Harper and Arianna get their story in LOVE, HONOR, and INK in the spring.

There are many Montgomerys, a few Gallaghers, and after that, a few secret surprises to come. Yay for bearded, broody, inked characters!

Montgomery Ink:
Book 0.5: Ink Inspired

Book 0.6: Ink Reunited
Book 1: Delicate Ink
The Montgomery Ink Box Set (Contains Books 0.5, 0.6, 1)
Book 1.5: Forever Ink
Book 2: Tempting Boundaries
Book 3: Harder than Words
Book 4: Written in Ink
Book 4.5: Hidden Ink
Book 5: Ink Enduring
Book 6: Ink Exposed
Book 6.5: Adoring Ink (Coming January 2017)
Book 6.6: Love, Honor, and Ink (Coming Feb 2017)
Book 7: Inked Expressions (Coming June 2017)
More to come!

Want to keep up to date with the next Carrie Ann Ryan Release? Receive Text Alerts easily!
Text CARRIE to 24587

About Carrie Ann and her Books

New York Times and USA Today Bestselling Author Carrie Ann Ryan never thought she'd be a writer. Not really. No, she loved math and science and even went on to graduate school in chemistry. Yes, she read as a kid and devoured teen fiction and Harry Potter, but it wasn't until someone handed her a romance book in her late teens that she realized that there was something out there just for her. When another author suggested she use the voices in her head for good and not evil, The Redwood Pack and all her other stories were born.

Carrie Ann is a bestselling author of over twenty novels and novellas and has so much more on her mind (and on her spreadsheets *grins*) that she isn't planning on giving up her dream anytime soon.

www.CarrieAnnRyan.com

Redwood Pack Series:
Book 1: An Alpha's Path
Book 2: A Taste for a Mate
Book 3: Trinity Bound
Redwood Pack Box Set (Contains Books 1-3)
Book 3.5: A Night Away
Book 4: Enforcer's Redemption
Book 4.5: Blurred Expectations
Book 4.7: Forgiveness
Book 5: Shattered Emotions
Book 6: Hidden Destiny
Book 6.5: A Beta's Haven
Book 7: Fighting Fate
Book 7.5: Loving the Omega

Book 7.7: The Hunted Heart
Book 8: Wicked Wolf
The Complete Redwood Pack Box Set (Contains Books 1-7.7)

The Talon Pack (Following the Redwood Pack Series):
Book 1: Tattered Loyalties
Book 2: An Alpha's Choice
Book 3: Mated in Mist
Book 4: Wolf Betrayed
Book 5: Fractured Silence (Coming April 2017)
Book 6: Destiny Disgraced (Coming September 2017)

Montgomery Ink:
Book 0.5: Ink Inspired
Book 0.6: Ink Reunited
Book 1: Delicate Ink
The Montgomery Ink Box Set (Contains Books 0.5, 0.6, 1)
Book 1.5: Forever Ink
Book 2: Tempting Boundaries
Book 3: Harder than Words
Book 4: Written in Ink
Book 4.5: Hidden Ink
Book 5: Ink Enduring
Book 6: Ink Exposed
Book 6.5: Adoring Ink (Coming January 2017)
Book 6.6: Love, Honor, and Ink (Coming Feb 2017)
Book 7: Inked Expressions (Coming June 2017)

The Gallagher Brothers Series:
A Montgomery Ink Spin Off Series
Book 1: Love Restored
Book 2: Passion Restored (Coming February 2017)
Book 3: Hope Restored (Coming July 2017)

The Branded Pack Series:
(Written with Alexandra Ivy)
Book 1: Stolen and Forgiven
Book 2: Abandoned and Unseen
Book 3: Buried and Shadowed

Dante's Circle Series:
Book 1: Dust of My Wings
Book 2: Her Warriors' Three Wishes
Book 3: An Unlucky Moon
The Dante's Circle Box Set (Contains Books 1-3)
Book 3.5: His Choice
Book 4: Tangled Innocence
Book 5: Fierce Enchantment
Book 6: An Immortal's Song
Book 7: Prowled Darkness
The Complete Dante's Circle Series (Contains Books 1-7)

Holiday, Montana Series:
Book 1: Charmed Spirits
Book 2: Santa's Executive
Book 3: Finding Abigail
The Holiday, Montana Box Set (Contains Books 1-3)
Book 4: Her Lucky Love
Book 5: Dreams of Ivory
The Complete Holiday, Montana Box Set (Contains Books 1-5)

The Happy Ever After Series:
Flame and Ink
Ink Ever After (Coming December 2016)

Single Title:
Finally Found You

Excerpt: Delicate Ink

**From New York Times Bestselling Author
Carrie Ann Ryan's Montgomery Ink Series**

"If you don't turn that fucking music down, I'm going to ram this tattoo gun up a place no one on this earth should ever see."

Austin Montgomery lifted the needle from his client's arm so he could hold back a rough chuckle. He let his foot slide off the pedal so he could keep his composure. Dear Lord, his sister Maya clearly needed more coffee in her life.

Or for someone to turn down the fucking music in the shop.

"You're not even working, Maya. Let me have my tunes," Sloane, another artist, mumbled under his breath. Yeah, he didn't yell it. Didn't need to. No one wanted to yell at Austin's sister. The man might be as big as a house and made of pure muscle, but no one messed with Maya.

Not if they wanted to live.

"I'm sketching, you dumbass," Maya sniped, even though the smile in her eyes belied her wrath. His sister loved Sloane like a brother. Not that she didn't have enough brothers and sisters to begin with, but the Montgomerys always had their arms open for strays and spares.

Austin rolled his eyes at the pair's antics and stood up from his stool, his body aching from being bent over for too long. He refrained from saying that aloud as Maya and Sloane would have a joke for that. He usually preferred to have the other person in bed—

or in the kitchen, office, doorway, etc—bent over, but that wasn't where he would allow his mind to go. As it was, he was too damn old to be sitting in that position for too long, but he wanted to get this sleeve done for his customer.

"Hold on a sec, Rick," he said to the man in the chair. "Want juice or anything? I'm going to stretch my legs and make sure Maya doesn't kill Sloane." He winked as he said it, just in case his client didn't get the joke.

People could be so touchy when siblings threatened each other with bodily harm even while they smiled as they said it.

"Juice sounds good," Rick slurred, a sappy smile on his face. "Don't let Maya kill you."

Rick blinked his eyes open, the adrenaline running through his system giving him the high that a few patrons got once they were in the chair for a couple hours. To Austin, there was nothing better than having Maya ink his skin—or doing it himself—and letting the needle do its work. He wasn't a pain junkie, far from it if he was honest with himself, but he liked the adrenaline that led the way into fucking fantastic art. While some people thought bodies were sacred and tattoos only marred them, he knew it differently. Art on canvas, any canvas, could have the potential to be art worth bleeding for. As such, he was particular as to who laid a needle on his skin. He only let Maya ink him when he couldn't do it himself. Maya was the same way. Whatever she couldn't do herself, he did.

They were brother and sister, friends, and co-owners of Montgomery Ink.

He and Maya had opened the shop a decade ago when she'd turned twenty. He probably could have opened it a few years earlier since he was eight years older than Maya, but he'd wanted to wait until she was ready. They were joint owners. It had never been his shop while she worked with him. They both had equal say, although with the way Maya spoke, sometimes her voice seemed louder. His deeper one carried just as much weight, even if he didn't yell as much.

Barely.

Sure, he wasn't as loud as Maya, but he got his point across when needed. His voice held control and authority.

He picked up a juice box for Rick from their mini-fridge and turned down the music on his way back. Sloane scowled at him, but the corner of his mouth twitched as if he held back a laugh.

"Thank God one of you has a brain in his head," Maya mumbled in the now quieter room. She rolled her eyes as both he and Sloane flipped her off then went back to her sketch. Yeah, she could have gotten up to turn the music down herself, but then she couldn't have vented her excess energy at the two of them. That was just how his sister worked, and there would be no changing that.

He went back to his station situated in the back so he had the corner space, handed Rick his juice, then rubbed his back. Damn, he was getting old. Thirty-eight wasn't that far up there on the scales, but ever since he'd gotten back from New Orleans, he hadn't been able to shake the weight of something off of his chest.

He needed to be honest. He'd started feeling this way since before New Orleans. He'd gone down to the city to visit his cousin Shep and try to get out of his funk. He'd broken up with Shannon right before then; however, in reality, it wasn't as much a breakup as a lack of connection and communication. They hadn't cared about each other enough to move on to the next level, and as sad as that was, he was fine with it. If he couldn't get up the energy to pursue a woman beyond a couple of weeks or months of heat, then he knew he was the problem. He just didn't know the solution. Shannon hadn't been the first woman who had ended the relationship in that fashion. There'd been Brenda, Sandrine, and another one named Maggie.

He'd cared for all of them at the time. He wasn't a complete asshole, but he'd known deep down that they weren't going to be with him forever, and they thought the same of him. He also knew that it was time to actually find a woman to settle down with. If he wanted a future, a family, he was running out of time.

Going to New Orleans hadn't worked out in the least considering, at the time, Shep was falling in love with a pretty blonde named Shea. Not that Austin begrudged the man that. Shep had been his best friend growing up, closer to him than his four brothers and three sisters. It'd helped that he and Shep were the same age while the next of his siblings, the twins Storm and Wes, were four years younger.

His parents had taken their time to have eight kids, meaning he was a full fifteen years older than the baby, Miranda, but he hadn't cared. The eight of them, most of his cousins, and a few strays were as close as ever. He'd helped raise the youngest ones as an older brother but had never felt like he had to. His parents, Marie and Harry, loved each of their kids equally and had put their whole beings into their roles as parents. Every single concert, game, ceremony, or even parent-teacher meeting was attended by at least one of them. On the good days, the ones where Dad could get off work and Mom had the day off from

Montgomery Inc., they both would attend. They loved their kids.

He loved being a Montgomery.

The sound of Sloane's needle buzzing as he sang whatever tune played in his head made Austin grin. And he fucking *loved* his shop.

Every bare brick and block of polished wood, every splash of black and hot pink—colors he and Maya had fought on and he'd eventually given in to—made him feel at home. He'd taken the family crest and symbol, the large MI surrounded by a broken floral circle, and used it as their logo. His brothers, Storm and Wes, owned Montgomery Inc., a family construction company that their father had once owned and where their mother had worked at his side before they'd retired. They, too, used the same logo since it meant family to them.

In fact, the MI was tattooed on every single immediate family member—including his parents. His own was on his right forearm tangled in the rest of his sleeve but given a place of meaning. It meant Montgomery Iris—*open your eyes, see the beauty, remember who you are*. It was only natural to use it for their two respective companies.

Not that the Ink vs Inc. wasn't confusing as hell, but fuck, they were Montgomerys. They could do whatever they wanted. As long as they were together, they'd get through it.

Montgomery Ink was just as much his home as his house on the ravine. While Shep had gone on to work at Midnight Ink and created another family there, Austin had always wanted to own his shop. Maya growing up to want to do the same thing had only helped.

Montgomery Ink was now a thriving business in downtown Denver right off 16th Street Mall. They were near parking, food, and coffee. There really wasn't more he needed. The drive in most mornings could suck once he got on I-25, but it was worth it to live out in Arvada. The 'burbs around Denver made it easy to live in one area of the city and work in another. Commutes, though hellish at rush hour, weren't as bad as some. This way he got the city living when it came to work and play, and the option to hide behind the trees pressed up against the foothills of the Rocky Mountains once he got home.

It was the best of both worlds.

At least for him.

Austin got back on his stool and concentrated on Rick's sleeve for another hour before calling it quits. He needed a break for his lower back, and Rick needed a break from the pain. Not that Rick was feeling much since the man currently looked like he'd just gotten laid—pain freaks, Austin loved them—but he didn't want to push either of them too far. Also, Plus Rick's arm had started to swell slightly from all the shading and multiple colors. They'd do another session, the last, hopefully, in a month or so when both of them could work it in their schedules and then finish up.

Austin scowled at the computer at the front of shop, his fingers too big for the damn keys on the prissy computer Maya had demanded they buy.

"Fuck!"

He'd just deleted Rick's whole account because he couldn't find the right button.

"Maya, get your ass over here and fix this. I don't know what the hell I did."

Maya lifted one pierced brow as she worked on a lower back tattoo for some teenage girl who didn't look old enough to get ink in the first place.

"I'm busy, Austin. You're not an idiot, though evidence at the moment points to the contrary. Fix it yourself. I can't help it if you have ape hands."

Austin flipped her off then took a sip of his Coke, wishing he had something stronger considering he hated paperwork. "I was fine with the old keyboard and the PC, Maya. You're the one who wanted to go with the Mac because it looked pretty."

"Fuck you, Austin. I wanted a Mac because I like the software."

Austin snorted while trying to figure out how to find Rick's file. He was pretty sure it was a lost cause at this point. "You hate the software as much as I do. You hit the damn red X and close out files more than I do. Everything's in the wrong place, and the keyboard is way too fucking dainty."

"I'm going to go with Austin on this one," Sloane added in, his beefy hands in the air.

"See? I'm not alone."

Maya let out a breath. "We can get another keyboard for you and Gigantor's hands, but we need to keep the Mac."

"And why is that?" he demanded.

"Because we just spent a whole lot of money on it, and once it goes, we can get another PC. Fuck the idea that everything can be all in one. I can't figure it out either." She held up a hand. "And don't even think about breaking it. I'll know, Austin. I *always* know."

Austin held back a grin. He wouldn't be surprised if the computer met with an earlier than expected unfortunate fate now that Maya had relented.

Right then, however, that idea didn't help. He needed to find Rick's file.

"Callie!" Austin yelled over the buzz of needles and soft music Maya had allowed them to play.

"What?" His apprentice came out of the break room, a sketchbook in one hand and a smirk on her face. She'd dyed her hair again so it had black and red highlights. It looked good on her, but honestly, he never knew what color she'd have next. "Break something on the computer again with those big man hands?"

"Shut up, minion," he teased. Callie was an up-and-coming artist, and if she kept on the track she was on, he and Maya knew she'd be getting her own chair at Montgomery Ink soon. Not that he'd tell Callie that, though. He liked keeping her on her toes. She reminded him of his little sister Miranda so much that he couldn't help but treat her as such.

She pushed him out of the way and groaned. "Did you have to press *every* button as you rampaged through the operating system?"

Austin could have sworn he felt his cheeks heat, but since he had a thick enough beard, he knew no one would have been able to tell.

Hopefully.

He hated feeling as if he didn't know what he was doing. It wasn't as if he didn't know how to use a computer. He wasn't an idiot. He just didn't know *this* computer. And it bugged the shit out of him.

After a couple of keystrokes and a click of the mouse, Callie stepped back with a smug smile on her face. "Okay, boss, you're all ready to go, and Rick's file is back where it should be. What else do you need from me?"

He bopped her on the head, messing up her red and black hair he knew she spent an hour on every morning with a flat iron. He couldn't help it.

"Go clean a toilet or something."

Callie rolled her eyes. "I'm going to go sketch. And you're welcome."

"Thanks for fixing the damn thing. And really, go clean the bathroom."

"Not gonna do it," she sang as she skipped to the break room.

"You really have no control over your apprentice," Sloane commented from his station.

Because he didn't want that type of control with her. Well, hell, his mind kept going to that dark place every few minutes it seemed.

"Shut up, asshole."

"I see your vocabulary hasn't changed much," Shannon purred from the doorway.

He closed his eyes and prayed for patience. Okay, maybe he'd lied to himself when he said it was mutual and easy to break up with her. The damn woman kept showing up. He didn't think she wanted him, but she didn't want him to forget her either.

He did not understand women.

Especially this one.

"What do you want, Shannon?" he bit out, needing that drink now more than ever.

She sauntered over to him and scraped her long, red nail down his chest. He'd liked that once. Now, not even a little. They were decent together when they'd dated, but he'd had to hide most of himself from her. She'd never tasted the edge of his flogger or felt his hand on her ass when she'd been bent over his lap. That hadn't been what she wanted, and Austin was into the kind of kink that meant he wanted what he wanted when he wanted. It didn't mean he wanted it every time.

Not that Shannon would ever understand that.

"Oh, baby, you know what I want."

He barely resisted the urge to roll his eyes. As he took a step back, he saw the gleam in her eyes and decided to head it off at the pass. He was in no mood to play her games, or whatever she wanted to do that night. He wanted to go home, drink a beer, and forget this oddly annoying day.

"If you don't want ink, then I don't know what you're doing here, Shannon. We're done." He tried to say it quietly, but his voice was deep, and it carried.

"How could you be so cruel?" She pouted.

"Oh, for the love of God," Maya sneered. "Go home, little girl. You and Austin are through, and I'm pretty sure it was mutual. Oh, and you're not getting any ink here. You're not getting Austin's hands on you this way, and there's no way in hell I'm putting my art on you. Not if you keep coming back to bug the man you didn't really date in the first place."

"Bi—" Shannon cut herself off as Austin glared. Nobody called his sister a bitch. Nobody.

"Goodbye, Shannon." Jesus, he was too old for this shit.

"Fine. I see how it is. Whatever. You were only an okay lay anyway." She shook her ass as she left, bumping into a woman in a linen skirt and blouse.

The woman, whose long honey-brown hair hung in waves down to her breasts, raised a brow. "I see your business has an...interesting clientele."

Austin clenched his jaw. Seriously the wrong thing to say after Shannon.

"If you've got a problem, you can head on right back to where you came from, Legs," he bit out, his voice harsher than he'd intended.

She stiffened then raised her chin, a clear sense of disdain radiating off of her.

Oh yes, he knew who this was, legs and all. Ms. Elder. He hadn't caught a first name. Hadn't wanted to. She had to be in her late twenties, maybe, and owned the soon-to-be-opened boutique across the street. He'd seen her strut around in her too-tall heels and short skirts but hadn't been formally introduced.

Not that he wanted an introduction.

She was too damn stuffy and ritzy for his taste.

Not only her store but the woman herself. The look of disdain on her face made him want to show her the door and never let her back in.

He knew what he looked like. Longish dark brown hair, thick beard, muscles covered in ink with a hint of more ink coming out of his shirt. He looked like a felon to some people who didn't know the difference, though he'd never seen the inside of a jail cell in his life. But he knew people like Ms. Elder. They judged people like him. And that one eyebrow pissed him the fuck off.

He didn't want this woman's boutique across the street from him. He'd liked it when it was an old record store. People didn't glare at his store that way. Now he had to walk past the mannequins with the rich clothes and tiny lacy scraps of things if he wanted a fucking coffee from the shop next door.

Damn it, this woman pissed him off, and he had no idea why.

"Nice to meet you too. Callie!" he shouted, his eyes still on Ms. Elder as if he couldn't pull his gaze from her. Her green eyes never left his either, and the uncomfortable feeling in his gut wouldn't go away.

Callie ran up beside him and held out her hand. "Hi, I'm Callie. How can I help you?"

Ms. Elder blinked once. Twice. "I think I made a mistake," she whispered.

Fuck. Now he felt like a heel. He didn't know what it was with this woman, but he couldn't help but act like an ass. She hadn't even done anything but lift an eyebrow at him, and he'd already set out to hate her.

Callie shook her head then reached for Ms. Elder's elbow. "I'm sure you haven't. Ignore the growly, bearded man over there. He needs more caffeine. And his ex was just in here; that alone would make anyone want to jump off the Royal Gorge. So, tell me, how can I help you? Oh! And what's your name?"

Ms. Elder followed Callie to the sitting area with leather couches and portfolios spread over the coffee table and then sat down.

"I'm Sierra, and I want a tattoo." She looked over her shoulder and glared at Austin. "Or, at least, I thought I did."

Austin held back a wince when she turned her attention from him and cursed himself. Well, fuck. He needed to learn not to put his foot in his mouth, but damn it, how was he supposed to know she wanted a tattoo? For all he knew, she wanted to come in there and look down on the place. That was his own prejudice coming into play. He needed to make it up to her. After all, they were neighbors now. However, from the cross look on her face and the feeling in the room, he knew that he wasn't going to be able to make it up to her today. He'd let Callie help her out to start with, and then he'd make sure he was the one who laid ink on her skin.

After all, it was the least he could do. Besides, his hands all of a sudden—or not so suddenly if he really thought about it—wanted to touch that delicate skin of hers and find out her secrets.

Austin cursed. He wouldn't let his thoughts go down that path. She'd break under his care, under his needs. Sure, Sierra Elder might be hot, but she wasn't the woman for him.

If he knew anything, he knew *that* for sure.

Tattered Loyalties

From New York Times Bestselling Author Carrie Ann Ryan's Talon Pack Series

When the great war between the Redwoods and the Centrals occurred three decades ago, the Talon Pack risked their lives for the side of good. After tragedy struck, Gideon Brentwood became the Alpha of the Talons. But the Pack's stability is threatened, and he's forced to take mate—only the one fate puts in his path is the woman he shouldn't want.

Though the daughter of the Redwood Pack's Beta, Brie Jamenson has known peace for most of her life. When she finds the man who could be her mate, she's shocked to discover Gideon is the Alpha wolf of the Talon Pack. As a submissive, her strength lies in her heart, not her claws. But if her new Pack disagrees or disapproves, the consequences could be fatal.

As the worlds Brie and Gideon have always known begin to shift, they must face their challenges together in order to help their Pack and seal their bond. But when the Pack is threatened from the inside, Gideon doesn't know who he can trust and Brie's life could be forfeit in the crossfire. It will take the strength of an Alpha and the courage of his mate to realize where true loyalties lie.

Love Restored

From New York Times Bestselling Author Carrie Ann Ryan's Gallagher Brothers Series

In the first of a Montgomery Ink spin-off series from NYT Bestselling Author Carrie Ann Ryan, a broken man uncovers the truth of what it means to take a second chance with the most unexpected woman...

Graham Gallagher has seen it all. And when tragedy struck, lost it all. He's been the backbone of his brothers, the one they all rely on in their lives and business. And when it comes to falling in love and creating a life, he knows what it's like to have it all and watch it crumble. He's done with looking for another person to warm his bed, but apparently he didn't learn his lesson because the new piercer at Montgomery Ink tempts him like no other.

Blake Brennen may have been born a trust fund baby, but she's created a whole new life for herself in the world of ink, piercings, and freedom. Only the ties she'd thought she'd cut long ago aren't as severed as she'd believed. When she finds Graham constantly in her path, she knows from first glance that he's the wrong kind of guy for her. Except that Blake excels at making the wrong choice and Graham might be the ultimate temptation for the bad girl she'd thought long buried.

Printed in Great Britain
by Amazon